A Shroud of Evidence

© 2009 By Glen C. Davis
Cover © 2009 by Glen C. Davis

Printed by Lulu.com

Published by Glen C. Davis
International Standard Book Number 978-0-578-01065-6

*This tale is dedicated to my Father,
who was a Christian when it really mattered.*

INTRODUCTION

I am writing this after significant internal debate. This is not a religious text, nor is it intended to be. I did not wake every morning to the sound of the voice of God saying, *All right, Glen, get this down*. Nor would I have you believe that God spoke to me and said, *Glen, I need some corrections to the original text*. What you believe is between you and God. In fact, I take seriously the words in Revelation, Chapter 22, Verses 18&19. Since I am not prepared to mount such responsibility on myself, I urge you not to use this book as any sort of religious teaching. Do not build any sort of theology around it. Reference the actual instruction manual.

On a secular level, it is a science fiction thriller. It is not intended to be sacrilegious and it is based solely upon my own imagination.

The events, people and compaies depicted in this novel are completely fictitious and any resemblance to persons living or dead is purely coincidental.

Anthony arrived at work in such a great mood that the harassment of the guards had no effect. That made them bitter which pleased Caine even more. He arrived at his desk with a clear mind eager to return to the drudgery of his work. It was a little after ten that he began to get an uneasy feeling. About half-past ten, he got scared. He was not allowed to keep certain files on his computer, but he had a good memory. Perhaps it would have been better if he hadn't slept well last night. If his mind was not so clear. Past verifications that he performed were coalescing in his mind with what he was verifying now. He was wishing that the information he now read was theoretical, but it wasn't. Long before "Dolly," this company may have cloned a lamb.

TABLE OF CONTENTS

CHAPTER ONE

*For many deceivers are entered into
the world, who confess not that Jesus
Christ is come in the flesh. This is a
deceiver and an antichrist.—2 **John** 7*

The human genome has been mapped. The American Genetic Research Laboratory led the way in the research; along with research in other areas. The laboratory sent a team of scientists with equipment to determine if a stain on the Shroud of Turin was blood or not. With a hefty amount of portable equipment the scientist determined that the spots were "probably not" blood. The report they produced gave no opinion as to whether or not the shroud was "as advertised."

Dr. Anthony Caine worked at this lab. His work was verification of various reports and statistics that passed his desk, though he did have a hand in some research. Dr. Caine entered, as he did every morning, and went straight to his desk. He picked up his Bible and picked out a passage to read. Dr. Caine had some apprehension about his work because of his beliefs. He used what he learned to attempt to prove his beliefs while others used it as proof there was no God.

"This is Dr. Caine, analysis," he heard a voice. "He's the token Christian. Gotta have one loser in every crowd."

Caine glanced over his shoulder toward the sound of the familiar voice. He found himself making a double-take. Alongside Dr. Kragger stood a brunette who was the cause of the second look. She was a young intern who was among the new arrivals from various colleges nearby. Caine examined her. Her face had the "new look." Every intern came through with that look of excitement and hope that they would cure some disease that wiped out millions a year, or find some new synthetic food that would stop world hunger. The "look" usually lasted a week, maybe two. The really enthusiastic ones might last a month. Sooner-or-later, the drudgery of the normal work day wiped that from their face. She was very attractive, but he was unsure of her beautiful smile.

"Hi, I'm Cynthia Darling," she said without approaching.

Caine turned back to his work in silence.

Dr. Caine was finished for the day He stopped at the security station on the way out to the parking lot. He laid his identification badge on the desk and placed his briefcase beside it. One of the guards opened it and quickly examined the contents. His colleague, having finished searching another employee, noticed Caine.

The name of the two guards who manned the station were Fred and Derrick. Caine thought of them as *Fred and Ethyl*. It was his internal rebellion to the daily ribbing that he endured from the two guards.

"Hey, Doc," the man grinned. "Talk to God today?"

"I talk to him every day," Caine replied without looking up.

"Really? Do you ever mention me?" the guard laughed.

"I pray for all lost souls," Caine replied. "It's my Christian duty."

Both guards laughed until a familiar, gruff voice cut them short.

"You boys are supposed to be concernin' yourselves with the security of the building. You can mock people on your own time. Which you'll have plenty of if you don't get back to work!"

The laughter of the guards subsided and Caine looked in the direction from which the voice came. At the edge of the desk stood "Sarge." Sarge was the direct supervisor of the guards and was notorious for his lack of a sense of humor. He was a short, muscular, balding man who commanded respect by his very mannerisms and seniority. He was on the job when Caine gained employment years ago. In fact, he was one of the few relics left from the time Dr. Richard Harold hired him.

Dr. Harold was the director of this institute and a friend of his. Unfortunately, he passed away two years after Caine was hired and Dr. Cornelius Devlin—who had been here longer than Harold—was elected Director by the Board. "The Board" was a mystery in itself. No one that Anthony knew at the institute ever saw a board member. They never met here, as far as Anthony knew. Anthony was not that interested in company politics, however, so he never really followed up on the matter.

Devlin immediately disliked Caine, for some reason. Because of seniority rules and practices, however, the worse he could do was relegate Caine to "desk duty."

To Caine, Sarge would always be Dave Carradine. Sarge was not exactly a friend of Caine's and Caine was not sure whether or not Sarge was a Christian. Sarge was just a professional soldier, so-to-speak, who demanded professionalism.

"You're clear, Doc," the guard interrupted Caine's thoughts.

Caine retrieved his badge and placed it in his briefcase. He closed and locked the case and picked it up. After a last glace at the guard, Caine left the building.

Caine pulled his key chain out of the pocket of his pants and with his fingers deftly singled out his car key. As he approached his antique '95 Corolla, he heard Cynthia calling him.

"Doctor Caine!"

He turned to see the young intern running toward him. He turned back and unlocked his car trying to ignore her. As he opened his car door, Cynthia was upon him.

"Hi, Dr. Caine."

"Is there something I can do for you?" he asked.

"Well, I was kind of wondering if you'd be interested in having a cup of coffee with me?" she asked.

Caine got into his car as he replied, "No, I don't think so."

"Why not? Are you Mormon?" she persisted.

"It's not a good idea to be seen with me," Caine said.

Caine closed his car door, started his car and drove away.

* * *

Anthony arrived home. He nodded acknowledgment to the manager of his apartment complex as he withdrew his mail from his box. He could hear his footsteps faintly echo as he walked toward his apartment door. He extracted his keys from the pocket of his pants once more and started to insert his key into the door knob. He paused for a moment as he began to sense something wrong. Slowly, he continued the ritual of unlocking his door. Carefully and quietly he opened it. He decided to leave the door open in the event circumstances dictated a hasty exit. He laid his briefcase on the table in the foyer and laid the mail on top of it. Quietly he peaked around the corners of his living room.

His eyes were abruptly drawn to a hideous hissing sound. Staring back through the dark from atop a bookshelf was two narrow, piercing eyes. A shadowy figure leapt toward him knocking down a jar of coins which fell to the floor with a crash. Anthony let out a sharp yelp and grasped at his chest as the dark, fuzzy figure slipped past him, through the door and out into the coming night.

"Mordred!" Anthony started to chuckle.

Mordred, a fat, black cat, was normally amiable in nature. When trapped inside the whole day like a prisoner, however, he registered his displeasure. Caine could certainly understand that. Tomorrow he would have to remember to put the cat outside.

After closing his door and making sure it was locked, Anthony sat down to read his Bible. It wasn't long before he was asleep.

Sometime during the night, he heard a mournful cry coming from a window. Mordred had returned. He rose up from the recliner and opened the door. Mordred entered and began rubbing against his leg as he closed the door and locked it.

"Oh, no. If you are going to be out partying all night long, you can just wait for breakfast," Anthony scolded and went to bed.

Anthony woke, showered, shaved and dressed. The only variation from this part of his morning schedule is that he did not shave on the weekends and, sometimes, not on Friday. He poured a cup of coffee and opened the box of stale doughnuts. He picked one up and let it fall to the counter with a thud. He would have to get some on the way to work.

He remembered to vary his morning routine enough to let Mordred eat his fill of a can of cat food. He was careful to remember to get him outside.

His morning ritual complete, Anthony made his way to work stopping to re-fill his over-sized coffee mug and pick up a couple of doughnuts. He parked in his usual space at work, which was near the outer edge of the parking lot. He did not rate a numbered space. He passed through the guard at the door and displayed his badge for *Fred and Ethyl* at the guard station. They were silent, but grinned at him.

Anthony went to his cubicle and sat at his desk. After reading a brief passage from his Bible, he set to work. About halfway through the morning, while making computations on some data sent to him over the network, he paused. There was something familiar about it. The title of the report, "Fishing Project," did not seem to be correct with the data he was reading.

"Don't you ever take a break?" he heard a voice from behind and turned to see Cynthia.

"Is there something I can do for you?" he asked.

"Can you take a coffee break with me?"

It was well-known that Caine did not break except to go to the bathroom. He comes, he works, he leaves became the running joke throughout the office. He was not sure if her persistence impressed him. For whatever reason, he set his workstation to password mode and rose. As he passed her, he said, "You're buying."

A few heads turned when they entered the cafeteria. Few could remember when they saw Caine in here last. Cynthia selected a wrapped conglomeration of chemicals—with just enough flour and sugar that the FDA would allow it to be classified as food—called a "Bear Claw." Of course, that was Caine's one morning weakness. Doughnuts were his usual breakfast fare. Caine grabbed a cup of coffee and waited at the check out. Cynthia met him there and their eyes met for the first time. She smiled at him. Her eyes had a slight twinkle that Caine found attractive. Cynthia pulled out a coin purse and paid the tab.

Caine felt slightly more comfortable with her as they moved to an empty table. When they sat, Caine studied her. Despite the fact that she bit into something only slightly resembling food, she was attractive. There was a suspicion lurking in the back of his mind.

"So," she said after flushing the substance down with coffee.

"So," he replied. After a pause, he finally said, "I can't help but wonder about the nature of this meeting."

"That's quite blunt," Cynthia replied. "Fair enough. I just wanted to get to know you."

"Why?"

"It looked like you needed a friend."

"Loneliness and I are old friends," Caine told her.

"Because of that Christian business?"

"I don't mind discussing my beliefs with people," Caine said, "if you, or whoever, are truly interested. But if you're out for a laugh—."

"I'm not laughing," Cynthia interrupted him. "I just thought you were— I don't know . . . "

"Pathetic?" Caine said.

"Perhaps. You look like you could use a friend. My parents were into all that Jesus stuff. It doesn't bother me."

Caine's apprehension was subsiding. He studied her and decided that she seemed sincere. Perhaps he could start a friendship. The fact that she was a female was a plus. He considered the fact that she was a very attractive female an extremely desirable factor.

"Well, I don't know, perhaps a movie and dinner," he muttered.

"Fine. Pick me up at seven on Friday," she said.

"That's pretty blunt," he replied.

She stood and smiled at him.

"You're buying."

* * *

The work week rolled on and Caine found himself wondering if the upcoming Friday was a mistake. Friday came and Caine sat at home watching the clock tick toward seven. He was considering whether or not to fulfill the commitment when he heard a knock at the door. He opened it expecting to find Gerald Cruthers. Cruthers was a reporter friend who lived in the apartments. Jerry made it a habit to drop in at the most inconvenient times to borrow things that Anthony really did not want to lend.

There, instead, stood Cynthia.

"Hi," she said. "Hope you don't mind. Thought I'd drop by and see how you live."

"Well, I, uh . . . " Anthony's voice faltered.

"Are you going to invite me in?" she asked.

"Oh, yeah," he said and stepped to the side.

Cynthia entered and Caine tried to close the door behind her, but it met with some resistance. He looked back to see Jerry forcing the door open. Before he could say a word, he forced his way past Anthony muttering, "Hey, Tony."

Anthony shook his head and closed the door. Cynthia turned and was startled to see Jerry leaning against the wall behind her.

"Why don't you come in?" Anthony mocked as he walked by Jerry.

"Tony, where are your manners? I've been here thirty seconds and you haven't introduced us," Jerry said.

"Jerry, Cynthia. Cynthia, this is a scum-sucking leech who lives in the apartment building. He can afford to because he never buys food while I'm stocked up," Anthony said with only a hint of humor in his voice.

"Cynthia, eh?" Jerry returned her smile. "I'm Jerry Cruthers, ace reporter for the Herald. You might have seen my work."

"Look in the recipe section," Anthony commented. "What do you want, Jerry?"

"I was wondering if I could borrow a little sugar," he replied.

Anthony sighed. "You know where it is."

"Not from you," Jerry said. "From her."

"Sorry, I'm taken," Cynthia said.

"You, my dear lady, are destined for a life of boredom."

"That's a chance I'll have to take," she giggled as she patted him on the cheek.

Cynthia went into the living room and was assailed by yet another intruder. Mordred had found her leg and was rubbing against it.

"What a beautiful cat," she commented.

She lifted him up and hugged him as she sat down in the recliner.

"Come on, Jerry. What do you want?" Anthony persisted.

"Did you hypnotize her down at that lab of yours? You working on some weird chemicals or something?" Jerry asked. "She actually chose you over me?"

"Could it possibly be your personality?" Caine suggested with a shrug. "What can I do for you?"

"Oh, yeah. You remember that cop friend of mine? He's working on a case and wondered if you could look over something for him. Some gal got killed and he thinks there is a coverup. One of the suspects is very important and he's trying to prove a rape and murder. If he can match DNA he thinks he can press for the prosecution of this guy," Jerry finished.

"When?"

"Tomorrow, if possible. I'll get an exclusive out of it," Jerry hinted at begging.

"Sure. Always glad to help the long arm of the law. And my arm is glad to show you the door."

"Thanks," Jerry said and looked over at Cynthia.

Cynthia smiled and waved.

Jerry shook his head and turned back to Anthony.

"Look. If this works out between you two, how's about seeing if she's got a sister. If not, give her my number, eh?"

"My sister's thirteen years old," Cynthia said.

"Wow. Good hearing," Jerry commented and left.

Cynthia stood and walked to Anthony.

"Sorry about that," Anthony told her as she approached.

"That's all right. I get creeps like that all the time," she replied. "Shall we go?"

"Where?"

"There's a science fiction retrospective at the Bijou," she suggested.

"I guess that's what I get for going out with a scientist," he said as he walked out of the apartment.

* * *

They sat in the darkness of the Bijou as the flickering light gave life to the screen. Anthony looked at Cynthia. She wore glasses to view the screen and stuffed kernels of popcorn into her mouth as the Martians of the 1953 movie, The War of the Worlds, attacked with their heat rays chasing a couple into an abandon farm house. The film had not been updated for modern release in some time, so the aging equipment of the Bijou was perfect for a retrospective. The glasses somehow made Cynthia more appealing.

Anthony looked up as the girl in the film began to cry and uttered,

"Oh, I could bawl my head off!"

The man on the screen responded to her plight.

"You're not going to. You're not the kind. Look. You're tired. You've been up all night. You cracked up in a plane; you slept in a ditch. You want to know something? It doesn't show on you at all."

"Now, why do they do that?" Cynthia asked without looking away from the screen. "What makes him think that with the world crashing down around them and the Martians all around that she's going to be concerned whether or not her lipstick is smeared?"

"When we are in similar circumstances," Anthony whispered, "I'll remember to tell you that you look like crap."

Cynthia looked over at him and grinned. "I knew you cared."

After the movie, the couple decided to stop at a Chinese restaurant. Anthony watched as Cynthia dug into her chow mein and egg rolls. It somewhat amazed him after watching her consume a large popcorn, soda, and a box of *Milk Duds* and *Bon Bons*. She paused and looked up at him. She swallowed.

"Didn't have lunch," she told him.

"I just don't get it. You don't eat like that normally, do you?"

"No. Normally I have pizza or burgers for dinner."

"How do you stay so. . . So. . ."

"You can say good looking now. We're not in danger of immediate death," she chuckled.

He smiled and started picking at his food.

"That's the first smile I got. I like it."

The slowly smile faded from his face. Cynthia paused stuffing food into her face to study him, but continued chewing the remainder in her mouth.

"Is there something wrong?" she asked.

"I'm sorry. I'm just not used to this. I mean— Well, this isn't a joke is it? I'm sorry, but I just have the feeling that I'll show up to work Monday to jokes from that group of idiots we work with.

"So you think this is a set up?" she asked.

"Sorry to sound so paranoid."

"Oh, you're not paranoid. I've had to listen to what they say about you. I'm hoping they're wrong. You do like women, right?" she asked.

"Oh, yeah," Anthony said trying to calm down. "It's better than the alternative. I mean, can you image me and Jerry?"

That drew the intended smile from Cynthia and he returned the smile.

He picked up an egg roll and began stirring it in the mustard.

"There was a time before I was a Christian, after all."

"So what made you become a Christian?" Cynthia asked returning to her meal.

"I read Revelation in the Bible. When I was in college, I used to watch all the horror films and played all the role-playing games. So, I wanted to see what it was all about. Revelation scared the hell out of me," he said.

"Literally, or metaphorically?"

"Both," he laughed realizing what he had said. "Anyway, I started reading the rest of the Bible and there was just too much in it. I'm not exactly a regular church attendee, but I read enough to learn how to get to heaven."

"I don't know as I believe all that. But I'd be interested in knowing more about your theory."

"It's more than a theory to me," he said. "I'd definitely be glad to share it with you. I mean, like there is one thing that always impressed me. Think of this. If you can accept that there was a Jesus and he was crucified. If you were a member of the Sanhedrin—those were the priest who tried Jesus—you know the scripture from what we call the Old Testament. That is what they used to teach from. They knew all of the prophecies. If you were one of these priests, you know what the prophecy teaches about the payment for betraying the messiah."

"Judas, right?" Cynthia said. "He got, what, thirty pieces of silver?"

"Right. If you were one of these priests and wanted to prove that Jesus was not the messiah, would you not offer thirty-one pieces of silver? Or even twenty-nine? I mean, you know the prophecy predicts thirty pieces of silver."

"That's and interesting point. But how are we to know that he received any reward at all."

"Ah, there was a spy. One of the Sanhedrin was named Nicodemus who, it is believed, was a secret follower of Jesus. In fact, he went to Jesus earlier in the Bible to learn from him. He was there at the trial of Jesus. Even got brave enough to speak up for him."

"Wow. A scientist and detective."

"We both use logic. I think that's why scientists try to disprove the Bible. They like to think they're saving the world and are not the cause of it's destruction."

"So you think I'm a mad scientist bent on the destruction of the world?" Cynthia chuckled.

"It is a fearful thing to fall into the hands of the living God. But call to remembrance the former days, in which, after ye were illuminated, ye endured a great fight of afflictions," Caine said.

He looked into Cynthia's eyes. There was a moment of connection that Anthony had never felt. Finally he smiled.

"Hebrews Chapter Ten."

"So how do I fall into the hands of the living God?" Cynthia asked.

"Well, two key elements are that you believe the Lord Jesus died on the cross for your sins and ask forgiveness.

"It's been a long time since I've been able to talk to a woman so easily about this topic. I mean, not a Christian. Actually, it's been a while since I could talk to a woman about any topic," he said and without thinking he bit into the egg roll which collected a sizable glob of mustard. It took only a few seconds for the toxic mixture to take it's toll.

It hit his tongue first. Shortly thereafter, he thought the substance would eat through the rest of his mouth. He felt a burning sensation like never before and tears streamed from his eyes. He reached for his water glass knocking it over. He felt frantically around the table for the pitcher of water, found it and began to gulp it down. When he finished half the pitcher, he set it down and looked at Cynthia who was dabbing her wet clothing and laughing.

"Watch that Chinese mustard."

CHAPTER TWO

Caine went to his favorite church on Sunday. They hadn't seen him in a few Sundays, so they were a bit surprised. However, he did not seem to get the sermon, this time. It would have been better if his mind was not on other things. He had feelings and emotions he had not felt in a long time. He was, well. . . He was happy. People even commented on it at the end of the worship service. They said he seemed to have a glow about him. Caine went to sleep that night and slept like never before.

Anthony started Monday morning with an unusual fare of oatmeal, blueberries and a glass of milk. He decided, however, to delve into decadence by adding a hard boiled egg. He let Mordred out when he finished breakfast. He exited his apartment and waved at Jerry who usually left for his job about the same time.

"Good morning, Jer," Caine called.

"Two years and you've never said good morning to me. Did you get some this weekend?"

As he walked to the parking lot, a delivery truck pulled up.

"Hey, Anthony," the driver said without getting out. "Got something for you."

He held a package out so Anthony could grab it. Anthony took it.

"Thanks, Carl. You have a good one, eh?"

"You, too," the driver replied and drove off.

Caine looked at the label of the package. It was from an Internet computer company he often ordered from. He opened it and found the two 8-gig memory sticks he ordered. He put the flash drives into his brief case as he approached his car. He got into his car and dropped the outer wrapping into the passenger seat.

Anthony arrived at work in such a great mood that the harassment of the guards had no effect. That made them bitter which pleased Caine even more. He arrived at his desk with a clear mind eager to return to the drudgery of his work.

It was a little after ten that he began to get an uneasy feeling. About half-past ten, he got scared. He was not allowed to keep certain files on his computer, but he had a good memory. Perhaps it would have been better if he hadn't slept well last night. If his mind was not so clear. Past verifications that he performed were coalescing in his mind with what he was verifying now. He was wishing that the information he now read was theoretical, but it wasn't. Long before "Dolly," this company may have cloned a lamb.

Caine glanced around and no one was observing his cubicle. He knew the camera layout and how to disguise his movements. With one hand he reached underneath his desk and opened his briefcase. He knew the inside very well and how to reach the pocket containing his flash drive. Caine did not leave his cubicle much so he kept a large coffee cup at his desk which was perfect for obscuring any possible camera view of his USB port. Carefully, he plugged in the flash drive and started to download the information he was viewing onto it.

He pulled up ancillary data, to support the information, and downloaded it, as well. He would never be able to get all of the files he needed to tell the whole story without a major alert—and he did not have clearance for some of them—but he could download enough to allow the press to ask some very interesting questions. There would be an alert given to the network security people concerning the information that he was downloading because it was classified. It was a big company, though, and Caine knew that it would be a week, or so, before he had to worry about it. By then, the information would be in the hands of the press. The big question is if the press would believe it enough to print it.

Success.

As he was pulling out the drive, he heard a voice. It was a friendly voice that he, now, loved to hear. It still gave him a start that almost caused him to knock over his cup. He was able to conceal the small flash drive in his hand.

"How are you this morning?" Cynthia asked.

He looked up at her and smiled as he let the flash drive slip from his hand into his briefcase.

"I'm doing fine. And you?" he said as calmly as he could.

"I just wanted to let you know that I enjoyed Friday night. If you ever thought about going out again, you know, I'm free."

"That's a fair price. I'll keep that in mind," he smiled. "How about lunch today?'

"I'll see you about eleven?" she asked.

"Eleven it is."

Caine paused to take a deep breath as he approached the security station at the end of the day. He was always searched by *Fred and Ethyl* and it never bothered him before. Of course, this time he had to make an effort to act normal. As he approached, he thought of several tactics that he could use. Normally, he just grumbled. Perhaps this time he could yell and make a scene. Drawing attention that way might keep them off-track. When he made it to the station the guards grinned.

"Hey, it's the Christian boy," Derrick laughed as Caine put the briefcase on the counter.

Caine took a quick, side-ways glance at the monitors that the security guards were supposed to check. He could not tell what kind of view they might have had of his activities.

"Paul. You know he took out that new Cynthia Darling girl?"

"No," Paul replied as he opened the case and started to scan the contents.

"Wonder if he got any? Did you get any, there, Tony? Wolf. Wolf."

The comment quickly drew Caine's attention and ire.

"Come on, George. Tony, here, is a Christian. They can't get it up."

The welcome voice of Sarge broke up the jovial mood.

"Are you gentlemen finished with your harassment?" Sarge growled.

The two men shot up straight and turned.

"Hello, Sarge," Fred replied.

"Your jobs here do not depend on your harassment skills. Your jobs are to search packages and bags and make sure no company material leaves without permission. Are you done searching his bag?"

"Yes, sir," Paul said as he closed the case and slid it back to Caine.

Fortunately, the incident caused by these two idiots gave him the distraction he needed. Caine picked up his case.

"My apologies for my crew," Sarge turned his attention to Caine. "Their actions will be noted when raises are discussed."

Caine knew that Sarge wanted to get rid of these two, but was under the same constraints which kept Caine in his position. Caine simply smiled nervously and nodded, then walked out the door.

* * *

"All right, all right!" Jerry Cruthers yelled as he walked to the door in order to open it and stop the incessant pounding. He was surprised to find Anthony Caine standing at his front entrance. "Hey, Tony. What's up?"

"Can I talk to you for a moment? Are you alone?"

"Sure. Come on in."

Anthony waited for the door to close behind him. Jerry gestured toward the kitchen.

"I trust this has nothing to do with borrowing from me."

"I need to ask you a big favor."

Gerald assessed the mood of his friend and took on a kinder attitude.

"Sure. What do you need?"

"It's the kind of favor that could land you in jail. Or dead. I know you don't believe in the Bible—."

"It's not that I don't believe in it, necessarily. I just haven't found any evidence of it's truth."

"Whatever. I have some evidence that I need hidden until I'm sure of what to do with. It's the real book of Revelation stuff."

"What is it? Do I get an exclusive?"

"Yeah. You can have an exclusive. But we gotta hide it for right now?"

"Don't worry. I got a place for it. What is it about?"

"It would take too long to explain, right now. But I will when I figure out how we should present the information. But you don't have to do this. This is really dangerous. I suppose I could find somewhere else to hide it."

Jerry shook his head. "I got this kind of thing all worked out."

"I don't know if I should do this."

"That's okay. But if anything happens to you I'm opening the package. And if nothing happens to you, we open it together."

"Deal."

Anthony pulled out a small, unmarked cardboard envelope—that he picked up at the post office on the way home—that contained the flash drive. He handed the envelope to Jerry.

"Thanks, Jerry."

"No problem."

Anthony turned and left without another word.

* * *

Anthony woke the next morning and prepared for work, as usual. The only exception was that he did not carry his remaining flash drive. He really did not want to take any chances. He exited his apartment and made sure his door was locked. When he turned around, he noticed a dark blue car drive off. The car did not speed off. The driver simply pulled into traffic and headed away.

The windows of the vehicle had a limo-tint, so he could not see the driver. It made him panic until the morning quiet was suddenly disturbed by an incessant and annoying boom boom of bass speakers. Caine breathed a sigh of relief as he realized that the vehicle was driven by some misguided youth. He had to take care not to let his imagination—or his conscience—get the better of him.

He drove to work in the same manner as he did every morning. He listened to his favorite mix of Christian music which calmed him. After work, he could consult with his pastor to determine the best course of action with the information.

Anthony entered the building and received a slightly less salty greeting than before. These guys did not like to mess with Sarge, but the absence of their harassment would only last a few days. He was expecting an encounter with someone on the matter of the files he took, but he went right to work as if nothing had happened. He even made sure that he took out his Bible, for a few minutes, though he was too nervous to really read.

About lunch time, a voice shocked him out of his analytical little world. He would have jumped at any voice, but fortunately this was a friendly voice. He turned to look at Cynthia but could not tell if she had gauged his reaction adversely.

"You have time for lunch today? I have some news for you."

"Sure," Anthony said as he stood. "Let's go."

They decided on hot dogs and sodas so they could go to the park. They found a quiet, out-of-the-way place to eat. Anthony could tell that Cynthia was too excited to eat, so he decided to wait for her despite his hunger.

"I just had to tell you. I started reading the Bible each night after our date. I used to read it as a kid and listen at church, and all of that. But this time I really started reading. There are so many things in there that I am sure we could prove empirically, but it was just—Well, one night it just all came together. All of those things I learned about as a kid and thought about growing up. I went to a church down the street from my house and gave myself to Christ. I would really like it if you would go with me tonight to celebrate. And I'd like to start going to church with you on Sunday and learn what you know and—

"Well, I'm just excited. For the first time in my life, I feel whole and right."

She looked at Anthony who just stared back while his brain tried to assimilate the flood of information that she gave rather quickly.

"Well?" she asked.

"Oh, yeah," he said and reached over and hugged her.

They spent the next couple of days having lunch and discussing things other than the Bible. Their plans, their dreams and their hopes. He decided that he would take Cynthia out tomorrow after work. After all, it was Friday and he and Cynthia would have all weekend to get to know each other. Despite his crime, his world was coming together for the first time.

The next morning was the same routine. The attitude, however, changed drastically. Anthony was actually excited to go to work again. When Anthony arrived, he went right to work. He did not notice, until about 2 p.m., that Cynthia did not come to see him. He started to worry a little, but he did have her number, after all. It was not uncommon for new people to get caught up in some research project.

It was on his way out that he got really nervous. Devlin was there to greet him before he could reach the guard station.

"Let's walk, shall we?" Devlin said.

Devlin led Caine into a wing rarely seen by the average analyst. The heart of the factory. Where all the "good" that *American Genetics Laboratory* produced originated. The genetics lab itself. It was quiet as everyone had left for the day. None of the scientist were allowed to work alone and all had to be out of the lab by three in the afternoon. That gave them time to decontaminate, debrief and be out of the building by five. Devlin took Caine into the animal research laboratory.

"Look around, Dr. Caine. What do you see?" Devlin asked.

Caine shrugged.

"Animals."

"Animals," Devlin repeated with a smile. "I see life. You see, everything we produce, here, has some benefit for mankind. I know you are a Christian and I respect that. You must understand that your God gave us the ability to make children walk or hear for the first time. An old man see again. A woman's brittle bones become hard so she could walk, or even run, without fear of falling victim to permanent damage. Isn't that something?"

"Seems reasonable," Caine agreed.

Cornelius began to walk and Caine followed.

"You may not realize just how important your analysis is to our research, Doctor. Very important. You might say that you are a part of helping all of those people. Your remarkable accuracy, even in the face of crunch time, has helped all of those people.

"So much so, I might add, that your name has even been entered to move into this world. Oh, yes, my friend. The board is reviewing your record closely."

The world you struggled to keep me out of, Caine thought to himself.

Caine followed Cornelius Devlin into a conference room deep in the lab spaces. T. O. Clark was all ready in the room so Caine knew he was in trouble. Clark was some sort of security person. He was slightly taller than Devlin, but much more muscular. His long, brown hair hung down without impediment by braid or tie, but it all ways had a neat, combed appearance. He was rarely seen and no one talked to him.

"But that involves *trust*, you see," Devlin said as he sat at the head of the table.

Devlin gestured for Caine to sit and Caine complied. Devlin studied Caine with a smile on his face for some minutes. Finally, he spoke again.

"Where are my files?"

Caine realized that he had no need to lie. After all, he was caught. He decided not to delve into who was cloned and was less interested in any board member names.

"The files I retrieved had nothing to do with developing a pill for osteoporosis. You cloned a man and that is illegal according to federal law."

"Not illegal, my friend. Just not encouraged. And the fact is that we are a federally funded organization that is responsible—and reports to—the CDC on an annual basis. They have never had a problem with our research. Now I ask you again, where are my files."

Caine became silent. Devlin took a moment to calm himself and nodded his head. Finally, he stood up.

"I thought this might present a problem for you. So I brought in a little enticement."

Devlin moved a dressing barrier to reveal Cynthia bound to a chair and gagged. She looked frightened, but this all seemed too crazy. Could she have been spying on him? Or was her pale, frightened appearance a reality? Could she have been "in" with the boss all this time. Caine could not believe that they would go through illegal means to obtain the information that he stole. If this was really happening, it confirmed what Anthony all ready knew.

"You can't do this. You're crazy," Caine said.

Devlin withdrew a knife that he had concealed in his coat. Anthony could tell by the style of the knife that it was not the casual variety. It was apparent that Devlin was interested in more than genetics. He watched as Devlin ran the blade across Cynthia's throat.

"Perhaps this will help you decide. She is so beautiful, yes?"

Devlin moved the knife to various locations on her neck and began to make small nicks. Cynthia began to wince. If she were part of the plan, she was certainly earning her paycheck. Anthony was beginning to decide that none of this was worth guarding the information.

"All you have to do is give me my information and you both can be on your way to a tropical island, together, with enough money to live out your lives in privacy. As long as you agree to live in privacy and not become a media nuisance," Devlin offered. "I can make that happen."

Caine considered the offer. If he thought he could get away with this activity to retrieve the files, he probably could fulfill that offer. What *else* would Caine be buying in that package?

Devlin removed Cynthia's gag.

"If her blood letting doesn't convince you, maybe her words will. Go on, dear. Tell him what you want."

"Remember what I told you at lunch, Anthony. It's the truth," she blurted. "I read the last chapter. I don't understand all of it, but I do understand enough that I know you need to keep that information safe. Don't give it up."

Devlin looked stunned. He either thought that she would ask Caine to relent from fear, or was surprised that she turned on him.

"Cynthia, I—"

"What?"

"Yes," Devlin interjected. "What?"

"Cynthia I just wanted you to know that you look like crap."

All Devlin and T.O. looked stunned. Cynthia chuckled, and then began to laugh when she realized what he referenced. Devlin responded with a scream and jammed the knife into Cynthia's chest. It was quick. She gurgled, for a moment, then slumped forward as Devlin removed the knife. Devlin turned his full attention to Caine and moved toward him.

"Give me my information. Where is it! You know we'll find it eventually. Make it easy on yourself."

Caine continued to stare at Cynthia's limp body in disbelief. After a couple of minutes, Caine spoke softly and slowly.

"You took away my only happiness on this earth. You can only make me happy by finishing the job. God will take care of me after that."

Devlin jabbed the knife into Anthony's side. Anthony cried out and slumped to the floor.

"Where is it?" Devlin asked.

Caine refused to answer.

"Where is it?" Devlin asked again as he pushed the knife into Caine again.

Caine simply smiled. He watched as the knife made a final stab into his chest.

* * *

The door to the room suddenly flew open and Sarge entered.

"What the hell is going on?" he asked.

Devlin spun around toward Sarge, surprised by his entrance. He forgot that Sarge was the only security guard permitted to patrol this section of the laboratory and could do so at any time. He was quickly able to turn the surprised look into one of shock and horror. Devlin actually liked Sarge, but he knew what he had to do.

"I'm glad you got here, Sarge," Devlin said as he moved toward him. "This guy went crazy, or something. We came in and found him stabbing this young lady and then attacked he us. We had no choice."

"Just give me the knife, Sir."

"Sure," Devlin replied.

He reversed the knife and held it by the blade as he approached Sarge. When he was close enough, he flipped the knife through the air and drove it into Sarge's chest. He quickly retrieved it and stabbed three more times to make sure Sarge was dead.

"You know, you sure don't make my job easy," T. O. told Devlin after all was done.

"You're job is to find my information. You got it?"

"Sure, Boss. Sure."

CHAPTER THREE

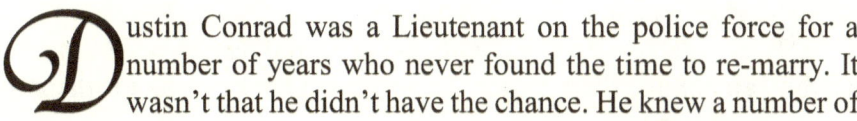ustin Conrad was a Lieutenant on the police force for a number of years who never found the time to re-marry. It wasn't that he didn't have the chance. He knew a number of

women. He watched others on the force that were married and chose to avoid the pressure. He was forty and there wasn't a grey strand on his head. He was still a few years from retirement, so he kept himself in pretty good shape for his duties and his latest girlfriend. At the moment, though, he was lacking in the girlfriend department. He carried an old .45 ACP on his belt, but his weapon of choice was his compact CZ-75, hidden under his coat, that was given to him by his father when he joined the force. He was wounded twice in the line of duty when he was younger and more apt to heal. Now that he was older, he preferred that the perpetrator be wounded. So he carried a couple of extra weapons if he thought he was going to be in a fire-fight. Today, he was simply on patrol listening to talk radio.

"I don't know why you Christians are worried about the chip," the guest chided the host.

"It's an evasion of privacy, for one," the host interrupted. "An abuse of government powers."

"Oh, come on. Your conspiracy theories aside, when has it ever been really proved that the government abuses their power?" the guest asked.

"How about destroying the bill of rights?" the host challenged. "The Second Amendment is gone. No guns for the citizens. You have lost sight of Federalist Paper #29, or choose to ignore it. What about the First Amendment?"

"You're on the radio. The government is allowing you to spout this crap over the air."

"For now. What about the Ninth Amendment? The Tenth? All of these are ignored or destroyed by law makers and their laws."

"Listen, we could go on, but this is about the chip. You Christians ought to be for it. Think of this. You aren't required to get the chip until you are old enough to drive. Therefore, your children will not have money on hand to buy drugs."

"And I suppose they will find no way around that. Remember the 'V' chip and other child video locking devices."

The guest chose to ignore the comment.

"They will have to go out with you to the movies, to eat, and so on, so you can control them better. There are no credit cards for them to steal to get cash. You will be able to control what your kids do, keep them away from drugs, and families will be closer together."

"Until you try to teach them about God. Then you are an enemy of the state and they take your kids."

"Oh, come on—."

The radio conversation was interrupted by a call. A murder at some corporation. Since Dustin was on duty, he would have to take it. He radioed his availability and turned at the next corner.

He arrived at *American Genetics Laboratory* as they were taking away a body. He stopped the coroner to take a look.

"Hey, Bob. Why did you remove the bodies?"

"These guys are all freaking out. There are chalk marks."

"Chalk *marks*, plural? Who are the *stiffs*?"

"One Anthony Caine, Cynthia Darling and a security guard named Carridine that got in the way. Apparently, this Caine, guy, freaked out and the boss and a security guard caught him knifing the girl. The security guard apparently got killed in a struggle. The boss apparently won the struggle."

"That's a whole lot of struggle. Who is the boss?"

"Dr. Cornelius Devlin."

"So do you buy it? What's it look like inside?"

"We haven't been in. That is the story that fella over there gave us. It's an FBI investigation, now," Bob rolled his eyes.

Dustin looked up to see the well-dressed, blonde-haired young man coming toward him. Dustin was not much into clothes himself, but he knew a tailor-made suit when he saw one. The young man displayed no outward sign of emotion.

"Is there something I can do for you?" he asked Dustin.

"Whose asking?"

The young man pulled a wallet from his suit pocket and displayed an FBI badge.

"James Colbert, FBI."

Dustin responded in kind.

"I see, Detective," the young man said. "Who called you in?"

"When you call for a coroner, you get a cop. Kind of goes with the territory."

"I see. Well, thank you for your interest, but everything has been taken care of."

"What do you mean, 'taken care of'. There has been a murder in my city."

"Well, yes, I understand, Officer. But this company does a lot of work for the government and, thus, this case is under the jurisdiction of the FBI. I'm sure you understand *national security*. Your department has been notified and a full report will be submitted within twenty-four hours, as required. You understand, I hope. We're not trying to step on any toes, but this does concern certain classified information. Need-to-know," Colbert explained.

Dustin surveyed the man, for a moment, then smiled.

"Well. That makes my job easier. Thanks."

"Good day, Detective," the young man returned the smile.

Dustin turned and walked away. He did not like being brushed off like a rookie. He got into his car and drove off with an uneasy feeling. He did not know Anthony personally, but they had met through their mutual friend. Anthony did some work for him when he did not want to go through police channels. On the few occasions they met, Anthony did not seem like the type to go nuts. There could have been some repressed matter, though. The only way to be sure would be to contact their common acquaintance.

* * *

Dustin turned into the parking lot of Anthony's apartment building and found an unobtrusive parking space. He took a route to Jerry's apartment that would not be visible by the possible investigators at Anthony's place. He knocked on the door and Jerry answered wearing his robe.

"Do you have a warrant?" Jerry asked.

"Funny. Can I come in?"

"Sure."

Dustin was not one to beat-about-the-bush. He began question-ing when he entered.

"I have a few questions about Anthony Caine."

"Tony? Sure. What do you need to know?"

"Was he depressed lately?"

"Not at all. In fact, he just recently hooked up with a girl that wouldn't have anything to do with me."

"Imagine."

"Yeah. They've been going out for a couple of weeks, now. Seemed very happy. Why?"

"Any other reason he might be depressed? In debt? Anything like that?"

"Not that I know of. What is this about?"

"He's dead," Dustin was blunt. "Was the name of the girl Cynthia Darling?"

Jerry had to sit.

"Cynthia was her first name. We never got around to the last name. Did she do it?"

"No. Apparently, he killed her—as the story goes."

"And you don't believe that?"

"I don't know. Something just bugs me about the matter and I'm trying to get to the bottom of it. If he were depressed, or something like that, it might fit. Any family?"

"His father left when he was about six. His mother is dead. No siblings."

For a brief moment, Dustin considered his childhood. His father left when he was young. If the lifestyle of his mother did not affect Dustin that way, however, he could not conceive of Anthony going crazy because of his past.

"Was he working on anything that you know of? Any new projects?"

"He did give me a package. It's at the drop spot. I can get it later."

"If you don't mind, I'll pick it up myself. It might be important."

"Just make sure I get the exclusive on the story. This could be big."

"Could be. And you will get all of the information that I have. I haven't let you down before."

"That's true."

* * *

The next day Dustin woke and conducted his normal routine. He showered and brushed his teeth. He forgot to shave and made his morning cup of coffee. While it brewed, he picked up a picture of his wife and grieved over it. His wife and baby boy were killed by a drunk driver two years ago on labor day. It was probably the only thing keeping him in his chosen profession. Though he was a detective, he was not above stopping and arresting every drunk driver he could find.

It was an hour before his scheduled duty time when he started his car and headed out of the driveway. He would get around to putting up a "for sale" sign. Someday.

He decided to head directly for the pick-up spot. He drove to the bus station on 12th avenue and found a parking space. In the afternoon, the terminal would be full and parking would be scarce. That is why he chose to pick up the package the following day.

He entered the terminal and glanced around. It was the same assorted mix of poor wretches that were normally there. Bus lockers were an old-fashioned means of transferring packages from one person to another, but they worked. The video surveillance was only good if you knew who had what you were looking for. He took out his key and went to the locker that it would open. He opened it and retrieved the small cardboard envelope purchased at a local branch of the post office. Dustin left the key in the lock and left the building.

Before going to his car, he looked around. He saw nothing. He just felt as though he should scan the area. He got into his car and drove away. As he drove down the street, he opened the package and found a flash drive. Dustin had seen flash drives before and knew what it was. He was concerned that it might be encrypted, so he drove to the home of another of his contacts.

When he arrived, he went to the front door and rang the bell.

He waited about a minute before ringing it again. He repeated the ritual about four times before he finally heard the grumpy voice on the other side.

"Okay! All right! Give me a minute!"

The door opened and revealed a man in a wheelchair. The man was about forty—Dustin knew forty-two to be exact. The man always had his long, grey hair tied back in a ponytail. He still wore the underwear he slept in with no shirt. Dustin used the services of this man for many years and knew he was slimmer before the avalanche that cost him both of his legs.

"What if I was your girlfriend."

"I only know of one ass that would wake me up this early in the morning," he replied as he turned his chair and re-entered his living room. Dustin followed closing the door behind him.

"What is it today?" the man asked.

"Well, Fred, I have a flash-drive that I need you to look over. It might be encrypted. Can you break it down for me?"

"Am I on the police payroll?"

"No. Just a favor. But I'll be glad to pay what it's worth."

"Minimum two-hundred bucks."

"Two-hundred!"

"Hey, I don't know what I'm getting myself into, here."

"Just a murder case."

"Just a murder case," Fred repeated. "Tell me anymore and that price might go up."

"Okay, okay. I'll be back this afternoon," Dustin grinned.

He handed the device to Fred and left. It was eighteen minutes after his duty started that he called in. It was, also, too coincidental that when he did, he was told to report to a most familiar address. He decided to go without siren or lights, but did rush to the apartment complex where Anthony once lived. Now, he visited to investigate the death of one Gerald Cruthers.

CHAPTER FOUR

*W*hen he arrive, he found the coroner and several patrol cars all ready on the scene. He entered without a problem since most of the precinct knew him and avoided him. They did not care much for him because he was a troublemaker. He always referred to that *old Constitutional concept*. It was a shame the President could not wipe the remains of that document from the mind of the people. Without the impediment of search warrants, and such, police could move much more swiftly to *protect and serve* the people. He did get further than previous presidents, though, having a sympathetic Congress at his disposal. There was still a remnant of Americans that did not know what was good for them.

Dustin entered and found one of the few friends that he had left on the force. He, too, was not happy with the new order of things, but Dwayne Cole had a wife and three kids to support. Dwayne was a large, lighter-skinned black man. He always looked like he was ready to rip out your liver. He worked out constantly and trained his kids in the martial arts, as well. They all showed the results in lean, strong bodies. While he appeared to be a mean person, he was, in reality, a gentle soul. He would rough up a suspect if he had to, but only in the defense of himself or others.

Dwayne was the first to see Dustin enter and went to him.

"Captain is here," he warned. "And he's in a pissy mood."

Dustin glanced around and noticed Colbert and a couple of others who were not from the precinct. One man did not fit the profile of an FBI man and he knew he wasn't on the force. The trench coat that the brown-haired man did not hide his muscular physique. *CIA?*

"Whose that?" Dustin nodded his head gently toward the man.

"Oh. FBI, or something."

"What are they doing here?"

"They are looking for some kind of information that the government lost."

"Well, Lieutenant Conrad."

They were interrupted by a gruff familiar voice. Dustin looked up to see the Captain gesturing for him. Dustin walked over to the hallway passing by the entertainment center. He quickly perused the titles of the films as he passed.

"What are you here for, Dustin?"

"I'm on duty, Captain."

"Yea? Well, we got this one. Have you got your new I.D.?"

"I thought that the implants were set for next month."

"By the first of next month which is just nine-days away. Just about every one else in the department has theirs. Don't you want to be part of the brother hood of police?"

"I'm in the union."

"The union agrees with the measure. It's federal law. All government employees should be implanted by the first of November."

"Well, sir," Dustin replied with a careful measure of sarcasm, "guess I'll *hop to it*."

"Look, man. I don't know why you are so resentful of me. I know I was promoted over you, but I'm just more ambitious. I'm not trying to be your enemy."

"Yea, I know, Captain."

Dustin decided to try to defuse the situation a little, but was more interested in the DVDs aligning the entertainment center. All exactly aligned and alphabetical.

"Interested in movies?" the blonde man had moved quietly to them and surprised Dustin.

Dustin grabbed a DVD and handed it to the man.

"Casablanca. Consistently voted number two of all time," Dustin said.

"And?" the man looked at him quizzically.

"Why doesn't he have Citizen Kane? The number one movie of all time?"

He was, of course, *jerking the guys chain*, as the old saying goes. What really interested Dustin was that all of the DVDs were in order. Dustin and Jerry had a prearranged signal; again, old-fashioned, but it worked. Someone was looking for something. Dustin turned to the Captain.

"Any idea what happened."

"You know, we've got everyone on this. Why don't you just go and hit hooker-town, eh?"

"Sure, Captain. Have a nice day."

Dustin turned and walked toward the door. As he did, he noted, with some interest, that the blond man opened the case of the DVD and examined it carefully as if there were to be some clue inside.

"Look around. See if you can find Citizen Kane," he heard the blonde tell another man.

He smiled as he walked toward the door. The Captain yelled after him as he left.

"You can take the day off if you want to go get your chip!"

Dustin drove for awhile before going back to his contact. He wasn't really that embittered over Captain Crane getting promoted over him. It was just that Captain Crane was a jerk. The man was not ambitious. He was ruthless. He worked just a little too closely with any one who would flash an F.B.I. badge. As if he were submitting a resume.

The chip, of which the Captain spoke, was the chip. The one that would allow them to track you where every you might go. There was a big push for all government employees—Federal and State—to get the implant. It was a procedure that took about thirty minutes—five minutes to prepare and give the injection and some time waiting to see if the body rejected it.

Dustin understood the logic, of course. Terrorist cells in the U.S. decided that the meteor strike in the Southeast was some sort of sign to react. And they did. Across the country a rash of bombing occurred. Glen Canyon Damn on the Colorado River was taken out and two nuclear plants were gone before Homeland Security could sufficiently react. It was decided, then, that all police agencies, people working at nuclear sites, the military, fire fighters and the like would
get the implant first so that Homeland Security could assess where everyone was so that they could react to a next strike more quickly. All other U.S. citizens were required to have the implant by November 30. It was all logical, of course, but at what cost to freedom?

Dustin was not the only antagonist to the new system, in the department, but he was the most vocal. He knew, though, if he wanted to remain a cop, he would have nine-days to make that decision. He actually had an appointment for October 31st, just in case.

Dustin did go through hooker-town more to remind himself of the degradation into which world the world had delved than anything else. Prostitution and drugs were technically illegal, but there were rarely arrests anymore. It gave the U.N. "peace keepers" something to do, after all. The police were now more interested in "terrorist" which included almost any one who spoke out against the U.S. Government and were resistant to the chip. The Internet was so registered, tagged, and connected through spy stations that "terrorists" were caught. There were few hackers, these days, and some brave enough to hack into one system or another to put up a dissenting page, but even these hackers were eventually apprehended.

Dustin passed Norman Park. It was an old and small park. Dustin remembered playing there as a child. There used to be monkey bars where, now, only a few poles remained. In his day, the trees were void of any indication of who loved whom. There were fewer buildings crowding up to the border of the park.

There was a crowd here today, but not a crowd of laughing children. It was a crowd around a man who stood on the edge of the defunct fountain waving a book in the air. Dustin did not have to see the title of the book or hear the words to know the intent of the man. The intent of the crowd was clear, as well. They had no desire to take the condemnation spewed from the mouth of this Bible thumper.

Dustin had a choice. He could leave and come back around to recover whatever was left of the man. If he called it in, it would take time to get any one here, if they responded at all. Bible thumpers were not the most popular people, these days. Especially in this area. A brick flying through the air and striking the man in the head made the decision for him. He had to respond to the plight of the man.

He put up his blue light and hit his siren a few times as he turned onto the park and drove toward the fountain. The man continued to wobble from the blow while still clutching the offensive material. The people were cursing and striking his car with clenched fist as it forced them aside. He tapped the fountain with his car and the man fell forward onto the hood. Fortunately, the man had the wherewithal to grab a hold of the wipers on Dustin's car. Dustin backed the car up, trying not to run over any one, while people took their last shots at the man he was trying to remove.

Dustin managed to carefully drive to a quieter area. He parked and turned off the motor. He got out and went around to the hood to check the man. The face of the man displayed the scars of time as well as the new indentation in his forehead from the brick. Dustin was now worried. The man had to be in his mid-eighties. That brick did little for his health. Dustin opened the side door. He gently lifted the light body of the old man off of the hood and placed him gingerly into the passenger seat. Dustin closed the door not worrying about the seat belt. The nearest hospital was ten minutes away if traffic could be avoided.

About two minutes into the drive, Dustin looked over at his passenger. The old man was looking at him and smiling.

"Don't worry, Pops. We'll be at the hospital soon."

"It won't matter."

"Sure it will. Just hang on," Dustin tried to sound convinced. "You know, Pops, that was the wrong place to preach that stuff. You know they have churches for that. I should, also, point out that you can be convicted of a hate crime. I could have left you and no one would have said a thing."

"No. You could not. *Speak, Lord. Thy servant is listening.*"

"What?"

"The Lord called, you and you answered. He will keep calling and you must answer. Positively or negatively. But you must answer. Where you spend eternity depends on your answer."

"All right, Pops, thanks. I'll keep that in mind. Right now you should just sit back and relax, okay?"

The old man took his advice and became quiet the rest of the journey. Dustin called ahead to have an emergency team standing by. When they reached emergency, Dustin jumped out of the car and hurried to the passengers side. When he opened the car door, he learned why the old man became silent. He stared in the passenger compartment of his car while the doctors tried to console him that there was nothing he could have done. He reached down and retrieved the Bible from the floorboard and set it on the chest of the old man.

"He's not going to need that," one of the doctors chuckled. "You want it?"

"That was his personal possession. He died for it. You keep it with him, you understand?" Dustin scolded.

"Yes. We will do that," one of the more experienced doctors glared at the youth.

Enough time had elapsed that Dustin suspected Fred may have found something. After lunch, he headed that way. He arrived at Fred's house and gave the customary knock at the door. Fred answered, as he always did, but did not look pleased. He simply turned his wheelchair around and re-entered his inner sanctum. Dustin followed.

"Well, what did you find out?"

"What did I find out?"

"Yes. The drive. What is it?"

"It's the kind of shit that gets people killed. And I want it our of here."

Fred picked the flash drive up and threw it at him.

"What do you mean?"

"Look. I don't want to get involved," Fred protested.

"Who's going to know?"

Fred chagrined.

"Okay. Two times I dragged you into court. But we got a rapist and a child molester out of the deal."

"All right, look. You ever hear of the *Shroud of Turin*?"

Dustin shook his head.

"Over the years, since the death of Jesus, Catholics have collected relics that they believe were associated with him."

"With Jesus."

"Yes. This was supposed to be his burial shroud. It wound up in a cathedral in Turin, Italy."

"Okay," Dustin shrugged. "What is a burial shroud?"

"In Jesus' time, the dead were wrapped in a cloth and place in tombs. I don't know, I guess to make sure they were dead before burying them. Jesus was no exception.

"In the late 80's, a group of scientist did a carbon-14 dating on a sample of the cloth. They dated it between 1260 and 1390. But they took the sample from a patch of repair work that nuns did because the shroud was damaged in a fire. Everybody laughed and the debate went on. That is the official story."

"This is all about a piece of cloth," Dustin commented.

"Would that it were. There was another sample taken from the shroud earlier. A sample having nothing to do with carbon dating. A DNA sample that was transferred to a subsidiary company which was developing a new technique for cloning.

"The problem was that this strain contained an unusual sequence that repeated every seven hundred and seventy-seventh time. They labeled it *GGG*. They tried to replicate it. Apparently the carbon from the fire did affect their sample because the best they could do is replicate it to a sequence that they labeled *FFF*."

"Duplicate? What do you mean duplicate?"

"I'm going have to find another church," Fred shook his head.

"Stay with me. What are you talking about? What do you mean duplicate?"

"I'm trying to tell you that they tried to *clone Jesus*. They failed. Their failure is still out there somewhere, but the information does not identify him."

"What subsidiary are we talking about?"

"*American Genetics Laboratory*."

Dustin paused to take a deep breath. Now he was scared.

"Now, if you don't mind seeing yourself out, I have to go find a church. And don't bother coming back, okay?"

Dustin followed the instructions.

Dustin decided to hold on to this bit of evidence for a little while longer. The truth was that he didn't even know how to proceed. He had heard of Jesus, of course. That was the name that was not allowed in school. The closest he ever came to church was The Charlie Brown Christmas Special that his mother used to watch on DVD. To learn that they actually tried to clone him, well—

As he drove aimlessly, he reviewed the facts. Caine, who worked at *American Genetics*, obviously smuggled this information out. He winds up dead along with his girlfriend. American Genetics is tied in with the Government and there are government agents clamoring over the crime scene. He gives the information to Gerald Cruthers to keep it safe. He's now dead. Now Dustin had the drive. If he turned the drive in, could he convince them that he did not know what was on it.

It did not take a thesis in criminology to realize his future.

He decided to check out a priest. He heard tell that what was said in confession was sacred and could not be revealed. Maybe he could get some advice there. Dustin turned into the parking lot of the next Catholic church he saw. He exited his car and locked it listening for the two quick tones that accompanied the action. He entered the sanctuary and looked around. It looked deserted. He had never been in a Catholic church and the stain glass windows made an eerie impression.

He heard a noise and saw a man leaving a small booth. He walked to it and entered. He sat down and a little window opened. There was a strained silence on his part. The man on the other side waited patiently.

"*Forgive me father, for I have sinned.* I saw that in the movies. Is that how it goes?" Dustin asked.

"That depends. Have you sinned?"

The man's voice was smooth and calm. Soothing. There was no emotion in it. For some reason Dustin expected an Irish accent.

"How long has it been since your last confession?" the man finally asked.

"I've never been to church, Father."

"I thought not. It's no sin to enjoy the ball game. I have to wait and watch the video."

Dustin sighed.

"Would you reveal yourself to me?" the priest asked.

The request surprised Dustin.

"Is that normally done?"

The window closed and Dustin heard the door to the other booth open. Dustin exited his booth.

The appearance of the man was not at all what Dustin expected. He wore denim jeans and an old plaid shirt with his priestly collar. He had boots, but a cowboy hat covering his shaggy, white hair and bolo tie was conspicuously absent.

"Don't worry. I get that reaction a lot. I am a priest, I assure you," he said.

"Are you still supposed to keep secrets?"

"Not since the lawsuits. Have you committed rape, murder or child molestation?"

"*No!*" Dustin replied indignant.

"Well, there you go."

The priest turned and started walking. Dustin felt that was an invitation to follow, so he did. The priest opened his office door and held up a hand to stop Dustin. He entered and quickly returned with a box in his hand.

"Come with me," he said.

The two men continued down a hall from the office of the priest to a side door. It was a cold night even for this time of year. Dustin did not pine for any of that global warming, though. Seems that they had enough to last a lifetime. Though the meteor strike last year caused less property damage than anticipated, it did enough. It wiped out Miami, along with most of the Florida coast, half of Cuba and many other Carribean nations. The biggest casualty of all seemed to be the weather. It shifted rapidly between hot and cold—mostly hot. The dust which still clung to the atmosphere gave the rising moon a reddish hue. Much less than it used to, though, in days past.

"I sense that you carry a heavy burden," the priest's calm voice broke the silence.

Dustin looked back at their surroundings to find that they had entered a courtyard containing a beautiful garden visible even in the dim lighting. In the midst of vine and tree, one could clearly make out the well-lit shape of a greenhouse.

"Are you still sworn to silence?"

"As I told you. It depends on what it is."

Dustin remained obviously hesitant.

"I will tell you why we are out here," the priest smiled. "You are a police officer, so you are familiar with such matters."

"How did you know I was a cop?"

The priest chuckled.

"Your mannerisms. Your suspicions. Your obvious powers of observation. Like you, we are trained to observe and study. Profile, if you will.

"No matter. The reason that I brought you out here is because the walls have ears. They are not supposed to be, but my office, the sanctuary and even our confessionals are bugged. Can't have those religious nuts causing problems from the pulpit, now can we?"

"Bugged."

"Yes. We started security sweeps ever since we learned that churches were being monitored. You know. As part of that *rumor of war* know as the *war on terror*."

"Talk to the people who died along the Colorado River. Or the people who died near the San Onofre nuclear plant. See if they think that the war on terror is a rumor of war."

"But there is no real enemy to face. Is there? There is no *front line.* We started out with a *war on organized crime.* Then they found a way to use organized crime. Some suspect even to kill a president. Then there was the *drug war.* And the CIA sold drugs to fund covert operations. Now there is the *war on terror*, which has turned into a war on the Constitution. I could go on about how that war really started."

"A priest conspiracy theorist?"

"And you are required by law to report me to Homeland Security, are you not? Damn the First Amendment, full speed ahead. There are a group of us priest who still quietly believe in the Bible even if the church does not. We sit and quietly, wait and watch."

"Watch? Watch for what?"

"For people who carry heavy burdens," the priest smiled. "Now that I have told you enough to get me ten years of prison time without a trial, I expect that you would be more apt to give me details of your plight."

Dustin sighed again.

"After all, I cannot help if I don't even know the problem. If it helps, I'll keep it a secret."

"All right. I came across this flash drive during an investigation."

"Flash drive?" the priest looked quizzical.

"You know. A flash drive. They record stuff onto it with a computer. Music and files and such."

The priest shrugged. "My music comes on records. I don't use a computer. I'm afraid my only modern convenience is a television with an HD converter box."

"When was the last time you were outside?"

"What is there outside that I need?"

Dustin took the flash drive out and displayed it for the priest. The priest put the box under his arm, took the drive and examined it.

"Very interesting. And this holds music?"

"This one doesn't. It holds information of a sensitive nature. No doubt secret."

The priest chuckled again.

"Secret information that confirms some of my *conspiracy theories*, perhaps?"

"*Touché*," it was Dustin's turn to chuckle. "But, you don't even know."

"And I don't want to," the priest laughed. "Letting my imagination run is much more fun. Anyway, it will all be revealed very soon."

"You don't understand. This is real Biblical stuff."

"And I would not understand *Biblical stuff*," the Priest replied with a smile.

The priest handed the flash drive and box to Dustin.

"That is why I brought this."

Dustin put the disk away and removed the top portion of the box to reveal a black book. He was familiar with the book as he had seen them before. The inscription on the cover was quite clear.

"A Bible?"

"I understand more than you may know. You wanted help. There's the instruction manual that God left. Everything you need to know is in that book. And the only other advice that I can offer is that flash drive, and its contents, will not protect you. You won't be able to use it to barter for your life. You might as well unburden yourself. Dump it in the next trash can that you see."

"You sound awful calm about this whole affair."

"The nice thing about this book is it won't spoil it if you read the ending. I know who wins," the priest smiled. "Might want to check out Matthew Chapter 24, Mark Chapter 13 and Luke 21 for a crash course."

"Well, thanks. I guess."

Dustin turned and started toward the door. He paused as the priest's voice raised slightly and became more somber.

"*Then if any man shall say unto you, Lo, here is Christ, or there; believe it not. For there shall arise false Christs, and false prophets, and shall shew great signs and wonders; insomuch that, if it were possible, they shall deceive the very elect.* Matthew 24. Take care, young man."

* * *

Fred was considering all that he learned today. He was considering what church would be best to attend. He wasn't very mobile, but he could get to his sisters in San Francisco. He turned to his computer to get more information on the shroud. For some reason, he started deleting the email addresses of his family and friends. He was not big on displaying family memorabilia. He ran a program that ensured that any deleted information would be permanently deleted.

Then he went to make some tea.

Being an invalid, he had little to do but take online courses. He was quite the computer expert and programed many of the safeguards for his computer himself. That is why Dustin used him. He was able to infiltrate many government computers and remove any reference to his family from them. Just a precaution, really. He only had his sister and nephew left that he cared about.

He returned to his computer and sat the tea next to the monitor. As he did, his eyes were drawn to the little window that flashed the message, Permanent Delete Complete. He took a sip of the tea, then shook his head.

"I'm probably just being paranoid," he thought.

He decided to get back on the Internet and look for information on the shroud. He read several articles and was engrossed in another when the annoying knock came at the door.

"That son-of-a—," Fred continued to curse as he wheeled toward the door.

He opened the door to reveal two men dressed just the way he did not like to see men dressed when they stood at his door.

"Mr. Garner. May we have a moment of your time?" the blonde man asked.

"And if I say no?" Fred asked.

The man just laughed.

CHAPTER FIVE

ustin decided to head for home for the night. This was all too much to assimilate in one night. He made a T.V. dinner and decided to watch the news. It was late, so the important stuff

was recorded, of course. He watched with interest as General Francisco Olivi—accompanied by the newly re-elected President —walked into the Senate, packed with senators and representatives, shaking hands while an announcer spoke. He began to wonder what the world was coming to when a foreigner was allowed to address the assembled Congress. He only knew of one other time when a non-politician was allowed that honor. When General Douglass McArthur was allowed to do so in an attempt to make President Harry S. Truman look bad.

"General Olivi, only the second non-American general to serve as the Supreme Commander of NATO, addressed the newly formed Senate, today. After serving only seven-months, the General laid down his arms to accept the seat as the next Secretary General of the United Nations."

The scene cut to the General standing in front of the Senate with the President sitting behind the General where the Vice-President normally sat. The Vice-President stood behind him.

"He drew a laugh," the announcer continued, "at the beginning of his speech."

"I try to speak English, but forgive, please," the Italian said. "My English no good substitute for yours."

"The General outlaid his plans for the future," the announcer continued. "A plan strongly rooted in peace."

The scene cut to another portion of the speech the General gave.

"I work with you Army, Navy, Air Force and Marine for only a short time. I grow to respect them and to love the United States. You people reach not across the aisle, but across the street, bringing two great building of august men and women into one, to bring the United States into a new *familia* of nations. You have suppressed oppression in your nation and help me to suppress the terror where ever she may strike."

He drew a round of applause from the Senators with that statement, but Dustin knew it was more applause for themselves. It took a lot of courage, he supposed, for them to bring in U.N. troops to patrol the streets and suppress legal gun sales. He continued to listen.

"Now while we have a tentative peace through force, I, in my new office, extend an olive branch to those who would be our enemies. I hopes that we can practice our religion with each other in peace."

The announcer continued as the scene cut to images of the General speaking with people outside the Senate building smiling and shaking hands.

"The General has all ready scheduled an open meeting between leaders of the Orthodox Jews, Muslims, Christians and Hindus for October 29—less than one week after he will take office. . ."

Dustin turned off the television and spooned out the last of the gravy in his microwave meal. He made sure to put the plastic utensils and the dish the meal came in into the recycle bin as the law required. No use adding to the misery with his boss not to mention the five hundred dollar fine that went along with the offense.

Dustin did not bother undressing. He simply laid on his bed and was considering the events of the day and what to do with the disk. Without warning, he fell into a deep, restful sleep.

The next morning, Dustin took his obligatory shower and shaved. He put on whatever came out of his chest-of-drawers next. He went to his car and started it up to drive to work. He had the Taylor District, as usual, so he could pick up breakfast there.

He checked into the precinct and was greeted by the Captain with unusually warmth and familiarity. He was accompanied by Dwayne Cole, who wanted to tell him something, but apparently could not in front of the Captain. Cole ran the morning muster, which Dustin was not required to attend. Sometimes he did, but today, he just grabbed his task sheet with the normal listing of people and businesses to rouse in the Taylor District.

The Taylor District was his beat. It was located in a portion of town in which cops did not like to go. They never went there at night. Dustin was known, though. Through a careful list of maintained contacts and a series of "missed" arrests, Dustin survived. He did not like to conduct police business in that fashion, but he was generally alone down here. And he knew that he was able to help a few teens change their direction. One kid that he knew, over the years, was now an officer in the Navy. Two were Army rangers and, at least, one entered the priesthood. There were several others that managed to lift themselves up, with his help, and move themselves and their families out of the Taylor District.

He spent a normal day "harassing" the hookers and threatening arrest and decided to head straight home in the evening. He actually worked a little overtime pulling a girl's dog from a storm drain.

A throw-away phone had become as necessary for a cop to carry as a throw-away gun. Monitoring cell phone conversations without a warrant was illegal since the 90's. With the exception of the FBI, NSA, CIA, and any other government agency that could fund the equipment. After finding what they wanted, they could always get a "warrant" later. It assisted them, greatly, to know which phone number to monitor. So it became popular for police—in addition to their issued phone—to obtain a pre-paid phone. They were monitored, as well, once the number got through the system. To avoid that, they simply purchased another phone when the "free" minutes they received ran out.

Now his pre-paid phone rang. There were only four possible callers to this number. One of them was dead. He checked the number and it was one he knew.

"Yes, Dwayne. What's up?"

"Do you know a Fred Garner?"

Dustin did not have to read the tone of the voice to know this was a bad question. He had a sinking feeling that his days of worrying whether he hit the recycle bin were coming to an end.

"Fred?"

"Don't tell me. He's dead. FBI says that it was with your .45 ACP."

"I didn't do it," Dustin replied.

"Relax. It doesn't take a genius to figure out that we got the FBI report a little too quick. You gotta get out of town 'til I can figure something out. They got an APB out on you."

"I'll call you when I can."

"Better let me call you. Is there anything else I should know?"

"I'm told that all you need to know is in the Bible."

Dustin hung up the phone. He was almost home, but turned quickly around to try to avoid detection. He turned the police radio on and headed back to the freeway to get back to the Taylor District. He knew those streets and the people and felt his best chance to find out what was going on would be there. Just as he got on to the freeway, he noticed a Highway Patrolman in another lane slowly moving up beside him. He stayed calm. Until the Patrolman recognized him. That's when he pressed the accelerator.

Dustin knew that he could outrun most of the cops on the road with his *Accura*. He was also aware that he could not outrun the police radio. He would have to run five miles of freeway to get to the Taylor District. Though he knew the district, itself, he never studied a lot of alternative routes to getting there. And there were no guarantees that he could get away once there. After only a half-mile, he looked into the mirror to note that two more local police cruisers had joined in on the chase. He jerked the wheel in time to fit between a semi and an old *Volkswagen* van. He almost lost it when a cry rose out from his back seat.

"What the—!" Dustin exclaimed.

As soon as he straightened his *Accura* in front of the Semi, he looked into the rear view mirror to see the head of a young man sticking up.

"What in the hell are you doing in my car?"

"I needed a place to sleep."

"Boy, did you pick the wrong ride."

Dustin twisted the wheel and slid into the right lane amidst the honking vehicles. The young man was flung back down into his seat.

"Apparently," he yelped as he went down.

"You can get out anytime. I'll stop when I can."

Dustin checked the rear view mirror, again, and saw another vehicle had joined the chase. It was not a police car. It was a dark blue car with limo-tint windows. He was afraid that he knew who that was. He knew, very well, why they were in on the chase.

The young man apparently heard the chatter on the radio.

"Is that one of those police scanners?" he asked.

"It's a radio. I'm a cop."

"A cop?"

"Don't worry. Don't have time to arrest you right now."

"Aren't you supposed to be the hunter and not the prey?"

"I took a bribe," Dustin said.

He quickly shifted lanes, again, but the blue car kept pace. There was a sudden burst of noise and the car shuddered slightly as the police helicopter abruptly passed directly overhead. The rules of engagement prevented him from using his 20-mm in this circumstance.

"Really?" the young man prodded.

"No. And you really don't want to know. Now shut up so I can concentrate."

He heard the tone that told him that he had a text message. He pulled out his pre-paid to check it out.

"What's that?" the young man asked.

"You sure are inquisitive. My friend is telling me that they are setting up a blockade at exit 147. They know where I am headed," he said as he put away the phone.

"So?"

"So, we exit now."

Dustin moved the wheel to the right and cut through traffic with just barely enough room to make the exit. He felt bad because some poor guy just trying to make it home from work had to swerve to miss him clipping one of the pursuing police cars. This caused a chain-of-events taking two other police cars out of the chase. He checked his rear view mirror to note that the blue car and two other cruisers were able to avoid the collision and continue the pursuit.

The blue car was obviously rigged with something and pushing hard to catch up. He watched as it slowly pulled away from the two cruisers and caught up with him. The driver was good. Every turn Dustin made was followed by the driver of the blue car with equal alacrity. This was no mere driver which caused Dustin to worry. The fact that they did not concern themselves with the rules of a high-speed chase caused Dustin to feel slightly scared. He panicked when they pulled alongside him and the passenger brandished a weapon. It was, now, clear that James Colbert drove the vehicle. He maneuvered to side-swipe the other car as two shots rang out busting the window in the rear, driver-side door.

He looked in his rear view mirror and did not see the young man. "You okay?"

"Yeah. I'm just going to lay here on the floor for awhile, if you don't mind."

The maneuver worked, for the moment, so he tried it again. The other driver did not back down from this intimidating game. He maneuvered, as well. The two cars collided and Dustin felt the worse of it. He wondered what that car was made of.

Dustin turned quickly at the next intersection and the other car continued on its way. He knew, though, that the other driver would take the next turn and back-track to resume the chase. In the meantime, the other two cruisers turned to follow him.

"Come on, Lieutenant. Pull it over. Let's end this," he heard a plea from one of the patrol cars.

He turned again and checked his rear view mirror in time to see one of the patrol cars smash into the pursuing blue car leaving them out of the chase. The helicopter, though, was now open. It positioned itself behind him ready to fire the 20-mm's that were installed. The young man popped his head up from the back seat.

"There's an aircraft heading toward us."

"Yes."

Dustin had a sinking feeling that he was not going to make the next turn. Normally, the police chopper was to fire low into the tires to stop the running vehicle. He had a sneaking suspicion that the pilot was instructed not to worry about such care.

"Is it a problem?" the young man asked.

"*Yes*," Dustin replied ensuring to inject enough sarcasm to make his point.

Dustin prepared himself for the blast. He could not even stop. If he did, that would ensure that the burst of fire would cut through his roof into the drivers compartment as the helicopter passed overhead. A burst of fire that never came. Dustin looked into his rear view mirror to see the helicopter careening into the ground. He hoped that the pilot and crew would make it out. They were just doing their jobs, after all, just like him.

"Doesn't seem to be a problem now," the young man commented.

If he could only shake the last cruiser. To his surprise, he checked his rear view mirror and saw the cruiser slowing down. It turned to go to the aide of the helicopter crew.

"Wow. Cool chase," the young man said.

"Yea. Cool chase. Now, just who the hell are you?"

"A guy who wants to get out of the city. Just like you," the young man replied.

* * *

A van pulled up to the carnage that the blue car was involved in. Devlin and T.O. got out of the van and walked up to the blonde driver.

"Have you taken leave of your senses?" Devlin asked.

"Just wanted to test my skills," Colbert smiled.

"Well, obviously they are lacking. Not to mention the fact that you are likely to bring the media into all of this mess."

"You could have chased him down," the blonde retorted.

"There is an easier way, you moron."

Devlin returned to his van. After T.O. gave the blonde a dirty look, he followed. Both men climbed into the van and Devlin grabbed his cell phone. He dialed a number and waited. A voice came on the line after two rings.

"How may we help you?"

Devlin typed in a code of nine digits and waited. He heard another voice after only a few seconds.

"May I have your code please?"

"Certainly," Devlin said as he took a notebook out of his pocket. "86965676. Captain Morrison. We need to stop and locate VIN 237HTO7934DBA7."

"One moment, Captain."

There was a short pause.

"Suspect vehicle 237HTO7934DBA7 at the intersection of 24th and Vine."

"Thank you," Devlin hung up the phone. "Let's go."

Dustin stepped on the accelerator several times, but realized that it would do no good.

"What's the matter?" the young man asked.

"They are onto me. My car is dead."

When the car slowed enough, the engine died. Dustin jumped out and looked around. He was soon joined by the young man.

"What now?"

"You go your way and I'll go mine."

Dustin noticed a used car dealership and walked to the lot. He looked through the window of a used Saturn. He knew how to get in, easy enough. He just was not sure that he could hot-wire it before the police arrived. An older black man soon joined him.

"You like?" the black man asked.

"It'll do. How much and how fast?"

"I've been listening to the police scanner."

"Oh?" Dustin became worried.

"Yes. I don't get good T.V. reception. Not much else to do. Actually, I just turned it on about a half-hour ago."

"So this is going to get ugly, I take it."

"You don't remember me, do you?" the man asked.

Dustin shrugged.

"Should I?"

"Don't suppose. But about a year ago, a cop I know took a bullet to get the guy that raped my daughter. Just a flesh wound, really. But a guy who's willing to do that I don't see as a murderer."

Dustin thought for a minute.

"Samantha Paine."

The old man nodded.

"You have a good memory. You don't want this one. Come 'ere."

Dustin followed the old man to a garage. Inside were two cars in various stages of repair and an ugly brown Chevy pickup. The man handed Dustin some keys.

"Don't worry 'bout the look. She's in good shape. I've been drivin' her for years. No electronics."

"Thanks, man."

"Now, get goin', boy. You ain't got a lot of time."

Dustin jumped in the pickup and started it. The motor revved loudly. He pulled it out of the garage with a screech and headed down 24th. He could pick up the freeway and get out of town. As he passed the abandoned *Accura*, a van pulled up to it with a couple of police cruisers.

* * *

The police immediately leapt out of their cars and began to search the area. T.O. began to search the car for the flash drive as Devlin scanned the area. Dwayne Cole drove up about the time that T.O. walked back to Devlin and shook his head. One of the patrolman returned and came to Cole to make a report. "Nothin' Lieutenant. We are conducting a house-to-house, right now. Checking all back yards, and so on." "Then you are wasting your time," Devlin turned to interrupt. "Lieutenant. I suggest that you and a couple of your men search that used car lot for any missing cars."

Cole did not like civilians interfering with police business no matter what their status or rank in the community was. He also knew the Captain, however. And he was aware of the sensitive nature of whatever they sought. He decided to comply so as not to get the Feds too entangled in the investigation right away. He could stretch it out to give Dustin time to get some distance.

"Sounds reasonable," Cole agreed. "Come on."

He and the other officer headed toward the used car dealership. Devlin waited until he was out of earshot.

"That's why I suggested it, moron."

Cole went to the dealership and found the Mr. Paine in his office.

"Can I help you, Officer?" the man asked.

"Maybe. I'm Lieutenant Cole. I'm trying to find out if any of your cars are missing."

"Missing. Why, I don't think so."

"Can you check?"

"Well, as you can see, I'm a small dealership," The man said as he went over to the window and looked out. "Still, I got about forty cars."

"Can you check your inventory against your computer?"

"Computer?" the dealer chuckled.

The man moved back across the office and rested against a file cabinet.

"Why a computer would get in the way of my good old-fashioned file cabinet. I've been in business thirty years, Lieutenant, and I do it the old-fashioned way."

Cole smiled as he realized that the man was trying to be helpful.

"Let's get started," he said.

The other officers involved in the search completed their tasks and gathered to assist Cole in checking the inventory. Still, it took an hour-and-a-half before they finished. On those occasions that permitted, Cole looked over at Devlin who was stewing. Eventually, Devlin and his sidekick went back into their vehicle and sat. At the end of the search, Cole went to Devlin's van. The door opened before he reached it.

"Find anything, Lieutenant?" Devlin asked without looking up.

"No, Sir. No cars missing."

"Do you have the name of the dealer?"

"Right here."

"May I have it?"

"Can't do that. Police investigation. Privileged, and all of that."

"Would you kindly find out what vehicle is registered to him? Or do I have to find out via your Captain?"

Cole knew the Captain was the trump card. There was little more he could do.

"I don't suppose that would be a problem," Dwayne replied.

He went to his car and called it in. He returned in about five minutes with the information. He knew better than to try to stall Devlin any further.

"The dealer owns a green 1989 Chevy pickup. License bravo, victor, charlie, 389. Hope that helps."

"Thank you, Lieutenant. Your cooperation is noted. Have a nice evening."

Cole knew that was his cue to move and the door slammed shut as soon as he did. The van pulled away.

As T.O. drove back to *American Genetics*, Devlin spoke.

"Get the word out through your FBI and CIA contacts. Look for a 1989 Chevy pickup."

"Don't you mean a green one?"

"The man is a dealer with a repair facility. He probably changes the color and plates once a month. Tell them to stop anything that moves and find my files!"

"Why don't you stop him with a phone call?"

"The truck is too old to have a computer in it."

"Should Officer Cole have an accident?"

"Not right now. I don't know if I can risk even those idiot Christian circulars catching wind of these files until they are safely in my hands and can be sure that they are not duplicated. We only have a short time to wait."

"Wait? For what?"

"You will see, my friend. When the time is right."

"Yes, Sir."

* * *

The delay gave Dustin plenty of driving time. As soon as he got out of town, he headed through the brush and out into the desert. The dealer's truck even included a lighted compass and reserve tank. He should be able to make it to Benford. Benford was a small town about three-hundred miles away. He could fuel up there. He took the flash drive out of his pocket and glanced at it. He really did not know why. It certainly would not give him any more information than he all ready knew.

Dustin slammed on the brakes as a sudden movement caught his eye. He dropped the flash drive and pulled out his CZ-75. Dust covered the truck as it screeched to a halt and the face of the intruder slammed against the back window. Dustin turned the engine off and leapt out of the cab. He stuck his gun to the head of the young man in the bed of the pick up who still had his face against the window.

"Are you gonna shoot me?" the young man mumbled as best he could.

"I should. Just what in the hell do you think you are doing?"

The young man slowly moved into a comfortable position.

"I told you. I needed to get out of town. You just happened to be going my way."

"Kid, you just don't know what you are getting yourself into."

"Oh, I think I do."

Dustin chuckled and holstered his side-arm.

"Fine. You can travel with me to Benford. Then you will disappear."

"Deal. If we make it to Benford, I'll leave."

"What do I call you besides 'kid'?"

"Ummm. How about Clarence. Yes. I rather fancy that. Call me Clarence."

"Great, Clarence. Get in the cab. It'll be a chilly ride."

Clarence joined Dustin in the cab. Dustin quickly looked around and found the flash drive and placed it back into his shirt pocket. He started the truck and drove off. He noticed that the fuel was low, so he flipped a switch hoping that it was for the reserve tank. The gauge shot up to almost full again, but he knew that the reserve tank would diminish quickly. He hoped it would be enough to get to Benford. He glanced at Clarence with a look of curiosity on his face. He suddenly realized what Clarence had said. If we make it to Benford, I'll split. Well, they would make it if the little blighter had to push.

"So, what's your story. Why did you have to leave the city?"

"Because I believe in God."

"Because you believe in God?"

"Yes. Haven't you ever noticed that there are not many people left in the city that believe in God? Many are fleeing so that they do not have to have the chip implant."

"I just went to a church before I left. There are still churches."

"How many people were there."

"Well, one that I saw. But it wasn't Sunday. And the priest was still there. He wouldn't be there if there were no parishioners."

"If you know the Bible, you know that you do not worship on just one day. You worship God every day in prayer and thanksgiving. He does have a few people that attend on Sunday, though. Those who do not have the means to leave. Those who are just awakening."

"What do you mean 'those who are just awakening'?"

"Well, you for example. You inherently knew there is something wrong with the chip. That is why you delayed getting it, true?"

"How do you know I don't have the chip?"

"Because if you did, you would not be running. The police would not be after you and you know there would be no where to hide if you had the chip."

That was logical. The chip contained a GPS tracking device. They could pin-point him anywhere he ran if he had the chip. This kid was sharp.

"Anyway, certain people are destined to stay precisely where they are. After all, if that priest had not been there, you would have not gotten the advice you sought. Now that you have left the city, you are about to see many wondrous and terrible things. Things that the state-controlled media won't report in the cities. You haven't told me why you ran. But I will bet you found out something unbelievable all ready."

Dustin decided not to confirm the young man's suspicions with an answer. He did not even have time.

A flood of light interrupted their conversation causing Dustin to slam on the brakes once more. He tried to shield his eyes from the intruding light and was able to make out three vehicles with floodlights pointed right at them. Several silhouettes moved quickly against the offending backdrop. Dustin's door opened and he found himself facing an AK-47. The passenger side door opened and another weapon covered Clarence. Clarence did not move. Only sat and smiled.

CHAPTER SIX

"*T*urn off your engine!" a voice demanded.

Dustin complied and the two men were pulled from the cab.

"Okay!" the same voice yelled.

The lights instantly extinguished, but left Dustin blinded. He felt himself being dragged a few yards and then thrown to the dirt. His eyes were adjusting, so he was able to look up and make out a figure sitting on the hood of the center vehicle that had stopped them.

"Who are you?" the man on the hood asked.

"My name is Dustin Conrad. I'm a cop."

"I'm Clarence," the young man offered with glee.

"What are you doing here?" the voice persisted as the person pointed his weapon at Dustin.

"I'm trying to reach Benford."

The group laughed.

"That's enough," yet another voice.

"But he's a cop," the person on the hood argued.

"And if he had said he was something else and we found out he was a cop, I would have killed him myself."

Dustin's eyes did not regain their full night vision, but there was enough light from the compartments of the other vehicles that he could see a man walk up, grab the barrel of the gun and pull it away from Dustin's head. The new man was obviously the leader. He was calm. He must have stood six-foot and his long hair, which Dustin thought was grey, was tied back into a pony-tail.

Sadly, he thought of Fred.

"What brings you out here, Dustin?"

"I was set up for a murder rap. Didn't feel like doing the electron dance, if you know what I mean."

"I believe it is still lethal injection in the city," the man said as he helped Dustin to his feet. "Out here, they use the Guillotine. Or some variation thereof. But, your point is well taken. You see Paul? He's the cop we heard about on the radio."

"Check 'im," Paul demanded.

The leader snapped his fingers and another man produced a hand-held device. It looked like one of the scanners the store used. He passed the scanner over Dustin's right hand, a few times, and then his forehead. A green light displayed each time.

"There, you see? No chip."

He handed the device back to the other man who turned and left. The leader turned his attention back to Dustin.

"My name is William Tyler. I run this rag-tag group of misfits."

"And what do you do?"

"We are a militia group. We protect people coming out of the city. Or destroy those who need it. Where are you headed?"

"Benford."

That drew another laugh from the group. William shook his head.

"You don't want to go to Benford."

"Why not?"

"Because it has been turned into a United Nations outpost."

"*U.N.?*"

"Yes. Your media does not cover what is truly happening out here. The U.N. has taken over several smaller cities throughout the country. They are really Chinese and Russian troops under the U.N. flag. They use the towns as airbases and places from which to strike. The people they haven't murdered they use as slaves and concubines."

"That's crazy."

William shrugged.

"Why don't you get some rest. We'll talk in the morning."

The next morning, Dustin sat by the camp stove reading the Bible he had been given. He understood the priest's reference when he read in Matthew, Chapter 24:

> *And ye shall hear of wars and rumours of wars: see that ye be not troubled: for all these things must come to pass, but the end is not yet. For nation shall rise against nation, and kingdom against kingdom: and there shall be famines, and pestilences, and earthquakes, in divers places. All these are the beginning of sorrows.*

He thought of Clarence when he read :

> *Then shall they deliver you up to be afflicted, and shall kill you: and ye shall be hated of all nations for my name's sake.*

Was that the reason he was leaving town? As if on cue, Clarence appeared from the brush.

"You've been out there awhile. I guess you had to go, huh?"

"What's that?" Clarence asked.

"Never mind. Want something to eat?"

"I could eat, I suppose. What have you got?"

"Rattlesnake."

"Rattlesnake? Really? I've never had that."

"Neither have I. But food is scarce, out here. That is all they had."

Dustin handed him a stick with a bit of the meat on it and took up his own.

"What's it taste like?"

"Chicken. It's supposed to taste like chicken."

Both men took a bite and chewed the meat. Dustin savored the meat as he chewed. Clarence spit his out and Dustin's face soured.

"Remind me never to eat your chicken," Clarence said as he kept spitting in an attempt to remove the offending taste.

"Oh, shut up."

William came to them chuckling and bearing two full plastic sandwich bags and two juices. He handed the juices to the two men who eagerly imbibed them. He handed them each a sandwich and sat down next to Dustin. He picked up the Bible and opened it up. Dustin noted that the man's hair was not grey, but a dirty blonde. It was longer than Fred's, but braided instead of tied into a pony tail.

"The boys told me what they did. That is kind of a welcome aboard thing"

"That is some welcome. Do many stay?"

"Well, if they do, they belong with us. Anyway, if you cook rattlesnake with the right spices, it can be quite sumptuous. You can't just stick it over a fire and eat it."

"So who are you?"

"You mean my true name?"

"That's a start."

"William Tyler. I left my real name behind several years ago."

"What's the deal with that scanner."

"Oh, that. I am a graduate from MIT. When I left, I stole that scanner. It was being designed to place in stores. They have them now. They scan your chip and know everything about you including how much you are permitted to spend. You know they used the recent disasters as an excuse to get the chip implant legalized. Can't buy food without it. Control the food and you control the people."

"By *they*, I presume you mean the government."

"We haven't had a government since Woodrow Wilson took office. We had the appearance of one. But the government has basically been controlled by a clandestine group that goes much deeper than our government."

"I sure have been coming across conspiracy theorist lately."

"A conspiracy is only a fact yet uncovered," William smiled. "You cannot deny that the government is flagrantly passing laws that violate the Constitution. Well, actually since the time of Wilson."

"You mean gun control laws."

"Gun ban laws, now," William corrected. "The whole idea of the Second Amendment was to keep the government at bay. Now that 'We the people' are basically limited to .22 caliber weapons, that is easy with armies armed with Mac 10's, grenades, armor and the like.

"That's only the most important violation. You, yourself, should be aware that search warrants have not been constitutional since the 1960's. And the 'Baby Boomers' that took over did not change the warrants back. They simply used the worthless paper against their political enemies.

"We now have 'Hate crime' laws which make it an offense to say anything that offends any one. That violates the First Amendment. You know, the First Amendment was not instituted to protect speech that we agree with. We all know that Neo-Nazis and the *KKK* are all miscreants. But they are American miscreants. They would get very little sympathy from reasonable people anyway.

"And yet we vote the same type of miscreants in office time-after-time. Or do we?"

"Now you are saying that the elections are rigged? Come on. They can't fool with the elections. It's too public. To easy for any one to access."

"They will let you access it. Because you will look at the *procedure* and say *Oh, yes. This looks quite all right*. They won't let some one like me access it because I understand computers. I'm a programmer. I can show you a hundred different ways to make a computer say exactly what I want it to. That's why I'm out here. That is why this little group of two-hundred men are out here."

Dustin took the pause as an opportunity to consider William's arguments. He did know more about this technical stuff than Dustin, after all.

"Are you a student of the Bible?" Clarence changed the subject.

"I've been reading Revelation. I am just about convinced that we are there."

"What would it take to convince you?" Clarence persisted.

"It wouldn't take much. One more sign, I suppose."

"Have you read much of the rest of the Bible?"

"Not really," William admitted.

"I encourage you to read the books of Samuel. *1 Samuel*, Chapter 22, Verse 1, in particular."

William flipped through the pages of the Bible. He read for a moment, then smiled. He read a little more, then closed the book.

"I'll take that under advisement," he said. "In the meantime, I encourage you to stay with us. We could use a couple of good hands."

Dustin removed the flash drive from his pocket and tossed it to William.

"Here's a little more light reading. It might contain your sign, if you can read it. As for your offer, I'll take it under advisement."

"We are not technologically challenged. I have a few devices. We'll be moving this afternoon. You might stick with us for a while, anyway. We could use your truck."

"Where are you going?"

"Those mountains," William pointed off in the distance.

"There is another group that is supposed to meet us there. There is water and fuel, so you'd be able to continue on from there, if you like."

"I think that would be a splendid idea," Clarence replied.

"And that's another thing that might keep me away. Nothing personal, kid, but there's something strange about you."

The young man laughed.

"Are you afraid of me?"

"Not you personally, but the idea of you. You are still too much of a mystery. But this group might be just right for you."

"Well, you decide. I have to go and check on preparations,"

William said.

He set Dustin's Bible next to him and stood and stretched. Then he left.

Dustin finally decided to take the offer and went to the caravan. He noticed, right away, that his truck was all ready loaded with supplies. The canvas that bundled the goods covered the cab. It looked almost like an old World War II truck that he saw in the movies. He went through the caravan and found William listening to the radio.

"How did you know I was going to go?"

William lifted a hand to silence him. His attention was on the radio announcer, so Dustin listened in.

". . .Secretary General took office today after his intense efforts secured a tentative peace along the Gaza strip between the Israeli government and Hamas. The Palestinian Organization said that it might consider recognizing Israel's right to exist for certain concessions which were not released publically, as yet. The right wing militia group Hamas does not seem to agree to the concessions, for the moment, but said that it will study the peace plan carefully. Secretary General Olivi was hoping to announce a lasting peace at his inauguration, but said that this is an important first step.

"In other news. . ."

William shut off the radio.

"Well, there you have it. *For when they shall say, Peace and safety; then sudden destruction cometh upon them, as travail upon a woman with child; and they shall not escape*," William said sadly.

"Let's get out of here."

As the other men turned to signal for everyone to start their engines, William turned his attention to Dustin.

"Sorry. I did not know they loaded you down. But we do need your vehicle."

"That's okay. I decided to go along anyway."

CHAPTER SEVEN

*T*he ride across the desert to the mountains would take about two days. They had to move slowly to conserve fuel and limit wear on the vehicles. Even though he was aware of that fact, Dustin still had to resist the urge to punch on the accelerator. He was getting bored. The convoy suddenly halted. Dustin and his young companion got out to see what caused the delay and found that one of the trucks was overheating. Theywould be delayed about an hour. Dustin decided to take advantage of the stop in the bushes.

Just as he finished his business, a loud noise shattered the calm. He looked out to see the men looking around with weapons pointed into the air. Dustin looked up to see a devastating site. Three attack helicopters flew low over the convoy. Amazingly, they did not fire a shot. The men of the convoy were, apparently, not anxious to provoke them. He was not familiar with the helicopter design. He was, however, familiar with the red star painted on various points of their fuselage.

When one turned in his direction, he ducked down. From the front, it reminded him of a rat. Two of the helicopters flew low on either side of the convoy slowly moving down the line of vehicles. When they got to the end, they rose into the air and faced each other. The two helicopters slowly moved down the line, again, then all three shot into the air and flew away.

Dustin came out from his hiding spot and sought William.

"What was that?" he asked.

"Those were Russian Mi-28's. NATO calls them *Havoc* helicopters. They patrol this sector."

"Why didn't they fire?"

"Russians are great pilots. And even though they have been Westernized a little, they still know duty and follow orders to the letter. They were not here to attack, though they certainly reported our presence."

"What were they here for?"

"I suspect that they were looking for you. This flash drive must contain something devastating."

"Oh, it does."

"Don't tell me. You'll spoil the ending." William turned to Paul, the man who wanted to kill Dustin the first day that he arrived. "Paul. Send a message to our contacts. Tell them that we cannot meet them at appointed time. We will rendezvous at the resort. Then split up the group and we'll take three directions getting there."

"Yes, Sir," Sam replied.

"What's going on?" Dustin asked.

"We've been spotted. We cannot risk exposing the other group we were supposed to meet. So we are meeting at a different location. If we split up into three groups, chances are one of us will make it."

* * *

T.O. entered Devlin's office without knocking. He was expected.

"What have you to report?"

"The hunter group is still searching. They've stopped several vehicles along the highway, but nothing so far."

"He's not going to stick to the highway."

"The only other thing that they found was a militia convoy. They've all ready reported it so that an attack group could take it out."

"Stop them."

"They all ready have plans to stop the convoy."

"*No*, not the convoy! The attack group. I want this scum alive. And he's in that group, more than likely."

"I all ready told you they searched that group and found nothing."

"Did they land? Did they question every one?"

"They have the latest sensitive equipment."

"I want them to land and physically check out the group. Then they can destroy it if they don't find him."

"Whatever you say."

"Yes. Whatever I say. Now get going!"

* * *

Lightning suddenly pealed across the sky. Clouds had been looming as they left, but gave no indication of anything like this.

Lightning shot up from the ground and into the sky ripping the air and creating thunder that sounded like an explosion. He read, somewhere, that most of the lightning bolts actually originated from the ground and rose up. He never had enough scientific curiosity to stand in a lightning storm and watch to find out. Now he had no choice. Dustin never went to war, but felt that it must be like this. The clouds darkened the landscape so much that the caravan had to use lights to see and the bolts of lightning were dreadful on the eyes. Dustin was scared.

Three bright lights appeared over the horizon. Dustin guessed what they might be. He looked at Clarence and noticed that his head was down and his eyes were closed. The only thing apparently holding him in his seat was his seat belt.

"Are you sleeping through all of this?" Dustin asked.

"Shhhh. Say nothing."

"What?"

"Quiet."

The three lights drew closer and split into six. As Dustin feared, the *Havocs* had returned; each having two extremely bright searchlights attached. This time, they fired. The heavy bullets ripped through the lead vehicle causing it to explode. The rest of the vehicles stopped and men got out firing weapons. Three larger helicopters landed behind them. It wasn't fear of the fire fight that kept Dustin glued to his seat, though. It was fear of the lightning. He could not remember seeing such a display.

He glanced to Clarence once more and he still appeared to be sleeping. Was he meditating? Or praying?

Dustin looked back at the melee and—with the assistance of lightning and the flood lights—saw troops exiting from the helicopters. The troops fired sporadically just above the heads of the militia men. Dustin recognized the tactic as suppression fire. Although they took out some of the militia men, their main goal was to keep their heads down and unable to return fire until they could close in to capture them. Dustin had the feeling that they were searching for him.

He watched as his new friends fell to the ground. Some of their weapons still spewed fireballs visible even through the blinding light of the helicopters. The militia men even managed to lob a few grenades, but the U.N. forces kept them down and kept edging forward. Dustin felt that his surrender might be the only answer.

Another sudden blast caught his attention. It wasn't the blast of a firearm, nor even a grenade. This blinding flash came from the sky with a deafening roar of thunder. Dustin's truck shook violently and, had he not had the windows rolled up, he might have been permanently deafened. The ball of lightning struck some of the offending troops who became engulfed in flames. A second ball hit striking another group who likewise perished. The men of the militia seized on the occurrence to rise and fire. Dustin saw the U.N. soldiers falling. Adding to the firepower of the weapons of the militia was yet another fireball of lightning.

The U.N. troops were trying to fall back to get into the transport helicopters. Dustin could not tell if any made it. The helicopters rose up to escape the combat with nature. The larger transport helicopter turned to it's side as if a gust of wind forced it out of control. It struck one of the *Havocs* and both tumbled down on to their own men in a fiery death blow.

The other two *Havocs* rose up into the sky as two of the militia men, who managed to get the right gear, fired two hand-held anti-air missiles after them. The two missiles struck one of the *Havocs* which seemed as though it went out of control momentarily, but began to fly away again.

There was another ball of lightning that struck the functional helicopter. It started spinning out of control and crashed into the other trying to escape. Both came crashing into the ground smashing into the transport.

Then there was silence.

It took a minute for Dustin's ears to re-adjust. He realized that it was not totally silent, but that he could hear the tapping of the rain against his window and the metal of his truck. As the flames from the wrecked vehicles shot into the sky, he could see flashes of lightning off in the distance. He looked over at Clarence who now rested against the passenger door with his eyes barely opened. He smiled weakly when he saw Dustin looking at him.

"You don't expect me to believe that you caused all of this,"

Dustin said.

"You associate me with too much power. Only God has such a good aim."

"You mean like *Thor*, or something?" Dustin joked.

"I was kind of hoping that you were getting something out of that Bible that you read. Now, if you don't mind. . ."

The eyes of the young man closed and he went to sleep. Dustin got out of the truck to find out what just happened. The rain was surprising. It was not cold as he expected. I was warm. It was lighter rain that he thought it would be, but the drops were big. He walked through the drizzle to locate William. He found him with a man who obviously had some prior medical training. They were tending to a Hispanic man who took a bullet in the shoulder. Dustin arrived just as the medic remove the bullet. He looked around to see men and women filling containers with water.

"What happened here?" Dustin asked.

"Pedro, here, took a bullet in the shoulder. Fortunately we have a combat-trained medic to take care of him."

"No. I mean this battle. Do you guys have some weapon I'm not familiar with?"

"Oh, that. I learned not to question God on such matters, It's good enough for me that he cares."

"Are you saying that God is responsible for this?"

"I'm a scientist. Have been all of my life. My Dad was a scientist. I've never found any proof of the existence of God. Right now, I'd bet on God with 100-to-1 odds. I guess that is what they call faith."

Dustin shook his head and looked back at the people collecting water. For some reason, a woman stood out. She was beautiful. Her long, brunette hair was much like that of his late-wife. But she was taller and a little chubbier. She danced in the rain with her vessel as if she hand never seen rain. With her was a boy of about ten-years of age. He was a few inches over the average for his age with the same hair as his mother, but cut shorter. Perhaps they reminded him of his own wife and child. Would his boy have looked something like that?

The boy looked toward Dustin and noticed his interest. He smiled. A bit embarrassed, Dustin returned the smile and returned to his truck.

* * *

T.O. was informed that some VIPs were arriving, so he knew that Devlin would be outside. He exited the building to find Devlin waiting as anxious as a child waiting to open a Christmas present. He went to Devlin and whispered in his ear.

"We still haven't found Conrad. Two of the hunter groups were completely wiped out by some freak storm. The group appears to have split up. We don't know which group Conrad is with."

"This is a joyous occasion. Please do not ruin it," Devlin smiled.

T.O. noticed a bunch of strange suits running around the compound. He knew that they were secret service who were securing the compound. He was surprised, though, when two vans pulled up and more suits leapt from them. Two limos pulled up, right after, and two of the suits immediately opened the limo doors when they stopped. From one of the limos, the President emerged with a couple of members of his cabinet, as T.O. half expected. Surprisingly, U.N. Secretary General Olivi emerged from the other. Devlin walked up to Olivi and shook his hand with enthusiasm.

"Mr. Secretary, I have so longed to meet you. Mr. President."

T.O. noticed that Devlin only glanced at *the most powerful man in the world* as if it were an after-thought to acknowledge his presence. The President simply nodded in return.

"They tell me that you have this process to cure virtually all disease," Olivia spoke with his accent. Devlin took the U.N. Secretary General by the arm, as if he were an old friend, and led him toward the entrance.

"Yes, sir. I would like to show you our facilities and explain everything."

At the end of the tour, Devlin led the entourage to a little used conference room. The conference room was stuffed with food and drink. While Devlin continued to indoctrinate Olivi, the President and his cabinet members turned their interest to the food.

"So, as you can see, Mr. Secretary, we can synthesize exact antibodies to the diseases that we face."

"I am impressed, Mr. Devlin. I am truly impressed and dare say that the World Health Organization would be anxious to join in your efforts."

"That would be wonderful, Mr. Secretary. Now, imagine the advancement we could make with cloning."

"Cloning a human? That is a little far-fetched for me. I don't see that necessity."

"Imagine that we clone an exact duplicate of a person. Our antibodies cannot stop the bodies aging process. Only slow it down. With a clone, we could replace bad hearts and lungs without rejection. People could live for hundreds of years."

"Existence becomes a bore when you learn everything," the Secretary argued with a smile.

"Imagine, then, the historic implications. We could clone figures from the past. Napoleon, Caesar, Plato. Perhaps we could find out what made them who they were."

"You paint a dark scenario," Olivi became somber.

"How about cloning the ultimate man of peace?"

"If you are referring to who I believe you are, then I must think you mad. I'm sure that the Pope would have an argument against that."

"I think, Sir, that I will be speaking with the Pope very soon."

"Well. As for the disease control, I believe that I can back you on that. But I cannot approve of this cloning. I must, really, be going, though. I have to return in time for the signing of the peace accord."

"Peace. *Peace*! In the middle east. I must admit, Sir, that I am impressed with your accomplishments. Finally, a lasting peace for Israel."

"Well, thank you. Good day, then."

The Secretary went to the President and spoke with him for a moment as they enjoyed a sandwich and tea. Devlin went toward them, but stayed a safe distance while they broke their fast. When they left, he followed them out and watched as they got into their limousines and departed the institute.

Now, he would be interested in the where-abouts of one Dustin Conrad.

* * *

The mud delayed their travel for a day and slowed their movement, for a while. William was not too worried. He revealed that it would take time for the U.N. to augment their loses.

Group "Bravo" had reached the rendezvous before them. They reported a similar astonishing battle. The rendezvous point was about five miles out of a small town known as Quinden. William sent a few men ahead to see if the other group, that they were waiting on, had arrived. Dustin decided to go in with the group, since he had no oath to follow the commands that William gave. William did not object, as Dustin thought that he might. Clarence, now wide awake, decided to attend, also.

When they entered, the men under William's command went on to locate their contacts with pre-arranged codes and signs. That did not seem to interest Clarence and certainly did not interest Dustin. Dustin wanted to see the new rural life. This town did seem to be turned into a base of some sort. As they passed by one house, three people worked in the yard. Dustin noticed a Chinese officer emerge and confront the man and two women on the quality of their duties. He seemed amicable, enough, just very authoritative.

As Dustin and Clarence passed by a small-town Baptist Church, they heard music and decided to enter. They did so as the music ceased. The preacher was a large man in both height and girth. With his short cut, jet-black hair, he looked rather young despite his horn-rimmed glasses. He was a powerful speaker with a booming voice and appeared very persuasive, even though he spoke with a stereo-typical Southern drawl that Dustin found annoying.

He began to talk about a "rapture" which confused Dustin. The preacher read from *First Thessalonians* claiming that it ensured that the rapture was near. Dustin whispered to Clarence.

"I do not remember reading anything about a rapture in the Bible, do you?"

"Why ask me?"

"Have you read the Bible?"

"Well, yes," Clarence admitted. "I just was not sure you were interested."

"Well, what about it? What about this rapture?"

"That was a theory espoused by a young girl in the 1800's. It wasn't taught before then."

"This guy is saying that Jesus is to return before the tribulation. Is he?"

"Look around you. Is the world not in tribulation?"

"But they are about to sign a Middle-East peace accord. Won't that settle things down?"

"Remember what William quoted about peace?"

"What about this rapture, then? Why is it being taught?"

"Unfortunately, people are seeking comfort. Remember what Jesus said to the disciples in Matthew 24? *Take heed that no man lead you astray. For many shall come in my name, saying, I am the Christ; and shall lead many astray.* I know you haven't had the time to learn, but if you read the Bible and connect-the-dots, so to speak, you will find that Jesus does not return until all these things come to pass. He comes to bring peace on the earth."

Dustin noticed that a young woman took an interest in their discussion.

"What about Matthew twenty-five verse thirteen?" she asked.

"*Watch therefore, for ye know neither the day nor the hour wherein the Son of man cometh,*" Clarence quoted. "As I explained, Miss, the Bible only reveals one second coming of Jesus. You should really review the Revelation of our Lord and Savior Jesus the Christ."

"What about *First Thessalonians*?" an older man asked.

"You are claiming some *secret* rapture where no one will be able to tell that it happened. And you use Thessalonians Chapter 4 as your proof? What does it say? *For the Lord himself shall descend from heaven with a shout, with the voice of the archangel, and with the trump of God: and the dead in Christ shall rise first: Then we which are alive and remain shall be caught up together with them in the clouds, to meet the Lord in the air:. . .*

"Who could miss such a heralding when *Yoshua*—O, I'm sorry—*Jesus* comes through clouds shouting with angels trumpeting? Consider a person visiting the grave site of a loved one. Their loved one suddenly stands up and say, *Hi. Sorry. Gotta go now.* I am pretty sure that God knows how to keep a *secret rapture* more *secret* than that; if

He were planning one. The only trumps sound in Revelation and it occurs near the end of the tribulation. If you look around, the tribulation is here. The one that you call the antichrist is risen. Although there is no mention of a 'the antichrist' in Revelation, the term is very well defined in the Epistles of John."

"Non-believers!" the young woman yelled.

"We have non-believers, here," the man added his voice with disdain. "Probably spies."

The voice of the crowd rose from a murmur to a roar. The next thing Dustin knew, they were face-to-face with the preacher. He held up his Bible.

"If y'all don't believe the word of God, you can just get yourselves down the road."

"I thought that the word of God was for all," Clarence smiled. "Anyway, we don't want to cause a problem. I was just answering a question for my friend, here. We'll leave."

The two men stood and walked to the door. Clarence turned and addressed the crowd once more.

"However, I will leave you all with these words. *If therefore they shall say unto you, Behold, he is in the wilderness; go not forth: Behold, he is in the inner chambers; believe it not. For as the lightning cometh forth from the east, and is seen even unto the west; so shall be the coming of the Son of man. Wheresoever the carcase is, there will the eagles be gathered together.* Matthew, Chapter twenty-four. If someone tells you that you have to go to someplace to be part of this *rapture*, please consider those words."

The two men left with the wailing voices of the people behind them.

When they stepped outside, Dustin turned to Clarence.

"Who is *Yoshua?*"

"That is the messiah's Hebrew name. Jesus is his English nickname."

The two men walked down the street and passed a park. The bird songs still drifted through the air as if nothing was wrong. To the birds, there was no occupying force. They were in ignorant bliss as was any dweller in a major city. Dustin thought about what might be on

State-controlled television tonight. Another situation comedy with whatever actor found favor with the government before the occupation began. Either because of their favor of the United Nations political views, or lack of concern for political views at all. As he was thinking on such matters, he realized that Clarence was amazingly quiet. An abrupt voice broke the stillness that he was so enjoying.

"You two! Halt!"

They turned to see two sheriff's deputies with a couple of U.N. soldiers approaching. Dustin realized that the sun was setting low on the horizon and they must be in violation of some sort of curfew.

"Run," Dustin said and both men took off running.

Clarence was amazingly agile, even for one of his youth. Dustin took a path through the park. It was an amazing design. Trees and shrubs had been cut so as to provide no possible hiding places. In the center of the park stood an old Civil-war era cannon. He turned to Clarence in an attempt to make some snide comment about being able to load the cannon and use it against his pursuers. But Clarence was gone. Worse, Dustin heard the whistles blowing; obviously to summon help. Response was quick in coming and Dustin was quickly confronted by three more U.N. soldiers. He turned around to see the others coming up from behind. Dustin quickly assessed the two American peace officers. One of their faces displayed a gladness that he was caught. There was something too anxious about his look. The other was a big man who looked extremely strong. He had the look of somcone just trying to do his job and not being too happy about doing it. It reminded him of Dwayne.

"Never a damn cop around when you need one. And when you don't need one. . ."

CHAPTER EIGHT

Wherefore let him that thinketh he standeth take heed lest he fall. There hath no temptation taken you but such as is common to man: but God is faithful, who will not suffer you to be tempted above that ye are able; but will with the temptation also make a way to escape, that ye may be able to bear it.—**1 Corinthians 10:12&13**

*D*ustin was thrown into a cell with several other prisoners. Most looked as though they belonged there. One, however, stood out. He sat in a corner quietly by himself dressed in what appeared to be old potato sacks. Dustin started toward him and the man looked up. His eyes were tired and his arms and legs were thin indicating that he had not eaten in some time. Was he a drunk? A bum? He definitely was of a sound mind and seemed to be studying Dustin as close as Dustin surveyed him. Dustin decided to let the matter rest, though he had a feeling that he would get no rest tonight.

The judicial system followed the Constitutional precedence of a fair and speedy trial very close, these days. Your trial was speedy. There were no longer any delays, no continuances, or any interest in assisting you in getting a case together. And fair, after all, is such a relative thing. That is where Dustin found himself the next day. Not at a pre-trial hearing. But at trial. The court system had moved, since the eighties, from the concept of best defense to the concept of the best defense you gonna get. His court-appointed defense attorney was a testament to that concept. It was the same one for every person who stepped before the judge. Dustin had never spoken with him about his case and the man said very few words for each defendant.

The young judge seemed disinterested as each case came before him. Perhaps dispensing justice was cutting into his tee time. He moved them through, quickly, having all ready made a decision before they got there. When it got to Dustin's case, the judge stalled.

"Now in the case of *Quinden v.*, uh. . . Damn it! Why is it that no one can get these names down?"

"He came in last night, your honor," the bailiff replied. "No one has had time to question him."

"Well, that doesn't matter. What's your name?"

"Dustin Conrad."

He noted with defiant satisfaction that the people in the court were stunned that he did not utilize the proper platitudes.

"*Quinden v. Dustin Conrad,*" the judge said as he scribbled the name in the paperwork.

The judge paused and looked at Dustin.

"Dustin Conrad. That name sounds familiar. Are you famous?"

"Sort of. I've been wanted for murder-one for about a couple of weeks, now."

The judges eyes brightened.

"Oh, you are *that* Dustin Conrad. Well, well, the Sheriff has caught us a big fish. Murder, espionage, flight. . . Say, you don't happen to be innocent, do you?"

"The evidence doesn't say so."

"Can you identify yourself?"

"Of course not."

There was a quiet gasp in the courtroom and even his defense attorney—who had yet to even speak—was appalled that he did have the chip, yet.

"Were you aware that November 1st was the deadline for implementation of the implant program?"

"I had an appointment, but something interfered with it."

The judge laughed.

"A defiant one. And impertinent, as well. Well, the law is clear. You failed to comply with a legal statute. I cannot ship you off, right now. I am required, by law, to sentence you to spend the next ten days considering what is required of you. You might consider how best to address a judge in his courtroom. If, in that ten-days, you decide to get the implant, it shall be done immediately. If you decide not to get the implant, other means may be used to persuade you. In either case, we can then ship you off for whatever other trial you may need to do. You are hereby remanded into custody. Next case, please."

With that, Dustin was whisked back to his cell with the other prisoners. He was kind of surprised to learn that the progress of implantation superceded even extradition for murder. What use would the chip be, after all, when the IV was stuck into his arm. The cell was crowded and he wasn't too sure that he was happy with the company. He was equally sure that they were none to happy with him. When breakfast arrive, he found out why.

The deputy brought in a bucket of muffins and a bucket of water. Like animals, the prisoners charged at it and fought over them while the deputy watched with pleasure. When all settled down, Dustin reasoned that it had become customary in this cell to allow the larger and stronger of the prisoners to get their fill of the food first. The rest was left to whoever could scrape for it. There seemed to be little choice.

Dustin noticed the lone man still setting in the corner watching the fight. He went over to the man and sat beside him.

"Not hungry?" he asked the man.

"Extremely. I haven't eaten in six-days."

"That long?"

"The Lord went forty-days without food. I can last a couple of more, I suppose?"

"You a Christian?"

"Guilty. An enemy of the State," he smiled.

"How do you put up with this?"

"The Lord said, *Fear none of those things which thou shalt suffer: Behold, the devil shall cast some of you into prison, that ye may be tried; and ye shall have tribulation ten days: be thou faithful unto death, and I will give thee a crown of life.*"

Dustin suddenly realized why the man hadn't moved. His legs were broken. Dustin became angry. He rose up and went to the man with the food bucket. He hit him in the back of the head and the man tumbled spewing the food from his mouth. He tried to recover, but Dustin hit him again. A third blow knocked him to the floor.

Fortunately, it took the second strongest man a few seconds to get over being stunned by the action. Dustin was well-trained in hand-to-hand, but he knew that *Hollywood* crap of taking on three assailants at once was just that. His first blow was to the solar plexis to stun the man. He gave the man several more quick blows to the head before finishing him with one hard blow. He quickly turned to be ready for anyone else, but no one else seemed interested in tussling for the food.

"What is wrong with you all? Don't you realize that a man is hurt over there?"

"It's muffin day," one of the weaker men said meekly.

"What?"

"Today we get muffins. Once a week we get muffins. The best meal of the week."

Had it degraded to this? Fighting over a bucket of muffins for the amusement of a jailer? Dustin grabbed a muffin and threw it at the speaker. He walked over and gave the lone man two. He distributed the remaining muffins to the rest of the prisoners excluding himself. Even the two he had just beat to get them. They did not seem too pleased at his offer, but, fortunately, a deputy came and opened the door.

"Conrad," he called. "Come with me."

The guard led Dustin through the precinct. It looked like any busy police station that he ever saw. There were piles of paperwork and frantic cops trying to deplete them—or, at least, prevent them from tipping over. There were *skaggs* and *skanks* and the rest of the evidence of the decline of Western civilization. There were informants trying to get more for their information.

There were others. Women crying as they were separated from their children. Children who would be sent to get the proper free education. There were well-dressed men and elders who only committed one crime. From the bits he gathered, it was because they refused to get the chip implant.

Dustin paused to look up at the digital televison on the wall. It was the only diversion in the room. It displayed a picture of Olivi touring the progress of a building project. He heard the reporter's over-voice.

"Today U.N. Secretary General toured the building of the first Jewish temple in over two-thousand years. Workers, here, say that the United Nations provided enough extra equipment that the temple might actually be completed in less than two months. Building supplies have been pouring in from all over the world, mostly delivered by U.S. and Russian cargo ships. Amazingly, there are Palestinian and other Arab Muslim workman working right along side the Jews to complete the project.

"Over there, right in the center is to be the Holy of Holies. The central chamber where only the holiest of priest may enter to, allegedly, talk to God. And, I suppose, that is the time that God asks for the rent," the reporter chuckled.

"It's happening. Right before our eyes," the guard brought Dustin back to his reality.

"What do you mean?"

"That Olivi. He brought peace back to the Middle East. Peace on earth. Good will toward men."

Dustin was suddenly struck by the admiration in the eyes of the man. As if he were gazing upon a god.

"Well, let's go. Gotta get you to interrogation."

The guard lead Dustin down a corridor. The corridor was more quiet than the rest of the building and darker. As they passed by doors, he heard the sound of beatings and the cries of helpless men. He had a sinking feeling this would not be like any interrogation he had conducted. The guard unlocked a door and indicated that Dustin should enter. He did so. The door closed and locked behind him.

Inside there were two sheriff's deputies. One was the strong, young man that had assisted in his apprehension. The other deputy he did not recognize—not that he should. There were, also, three U.N. soldiers in the room. The deputy that he did not know approached him. Dustin was busy staring him down, so he was surprised when he felt a sharp pain in his ribs when the man got to him. He fell to his knees. It was then that he saw the night stick that the man had concealed until he could use it to jab into Dustin's ribs.

It wasn't fear of the man that caused Dustin not to react. It was the guns of the three U.N. soldiers that were stuck to his head when he started to react. Two of the soldiers grabbed him and dragged him to the wall where his hands were chained over his head in medieval fashion.

"Isn't this a bit unconstitutional?" Dustin questioned.

The deputy went over to him and hit him across the stomach with the full force that the nightstick would deliver. Dustin gasped for air.

"Shut up! I'll tell you what is unconstitutional."

The man became calm.

"Now. You want the chip, don't you?"

"Not as much as you want a plastic surgeon," Dustin decided to become defiant.

He had the feeling that he did not have much of a chance anyway. His suspicions were confirmed when the deputy walked away smiling and nodded to the stronger man. The man he recognized took a position next to him. The young man had put on a glove, so Dustin knew what to expect. Though Dustin could tell that the man did not like what he was doing, he lifted Dustin up and punched him in the solar plexis. Dustin gasped for air, again.

"You know this all can be avoided. Just give a holler if you'd rather get the chip than a beating."

When Dustin could breath again, the young man gave him a clout across the jaw. He beat him for about five minutes—stopping for a minute or two to prod him about that damn chip. This beating ritual continued for at least an hour. The young man seemed relieved when the other deputy stopped him. They must have recognized that Dustin could not take much more. The lead deputy pressed a button on an intercom and spoke.

"Room Six. Come and get 'im."

Dustin was taken to another room where a lady in a white coat stood waiting. They sat him on a table and the woman examined him. She carefully and quietly cleaned up the blood and applied bandages. Like the young deputy, she did not seem too happy about having to work on people who went through this procedure. Probably because she knew she would have to do the same thing tomorrow.

Dustin was taken back to the cell. He walked over next to the man with the broken legs and sat down.

"Now you know how my legs were broken," the man said.

"Yeah. I don't know how you remain so calm."

"I have learned the Biblical concept of forgiveness, my friend."

Their conversation was interrupted by looming shadows. Dustin looked up into the faces of the prisoners that he beat up earlier.

"Say, we were just discussing the Biblical concept of forgiveness. I don't suppose that you boys would like to join in," Dustin said.

As the two men lifted him up, he mumbled, "I didn't think so."

The two men beat him and one of the lesser men joined in—probably to try to gain their favor. This beating went on for about twenty minutes. Dustin could barely see through the blood seeping into and burning his eyes. Old wounds were re-opened and there were a few new ones for good measure. He looked up at the cell door and saw someone standing there. He could not tell if it was a man or woman because of his blinded state, but he assumed it was an officer of some sort.

A guard brought a bucket and allowed Dustin to clean himself off and left him with a few pieces of cloth to hold to his wounds.

Dustin decided it was time to sleep. Right where he was.

When Dustin woke, it was dark in the cell. He looked around and saw the stars through the barred windows. He got up and looked around. Every one was asleep, but it seemed that one of the prisoners was missing. He looked over to the lone man. He was still there and, amazingly, still awake. He walked over to him and sat beside him. The two beds were taken up.

"You still awake?"

"I nod off, from time-to-time. It's hard to sleep when the pain starts up."

"What about that nurse or doctor. Shouldn't she bind up your legs, or something?"

"She is only required to give the minimal medical treatment to keep you alive, by law. To be fair, I do not believe she is a physician. I do not believe that she know how to fix them. " The man paused for a chuckle. "You know, the law is a funny thing. Sometimes, it is the letter of the law that is important. Sometimes, the spirit. Depends on how they want to judge you."

"You're a weird guy. What's your name?"

The man shook his head.

"My name is of no importance."

"It is to me. What do I call you? Weird guy?"

"It's as good a name as any. I suppose that you could call me Christian."

"Is that your name or profession?"

The man smiled.

"You'd better get some rest, now. You know what's in store for tomorrow."

Dustin took the man's advice and went to sleep.

As he predicted, Dustin was collected for another beating. He was taken to the nurse in—what he felt was—worse shape than yesterday.

The young man did not conduct the beating. It was another equally adept deputy. This time, though, they experimented a little with electricity and needles. They seemed to have a jolly time complaining about Christians and offering him that implant.

When he got back to the cell, the two men were waiting. He tried to sit down and rest. They actually let him for about an hour.

"Aww, can't you guys give it a rest?" he pleaded as they finally lifted him up.

Again, they stopped when that mysterious figure arrived.

How long had it been? His mind became numb to time after the third day of beating and torture which were getting more intense and longer. They seemed to know just how much of a beating he could take and still remain alive. Yet, he was not sure just how much more he could take. He was about ready to give into any of their demands.

He was still confused by the tormented look in the face of the young deputy who was obviously forced to conduct the beating. He was not sure if the doctor who treated him was totally happy about her role in the affair, either. Even through all of the torture, he still managed to pity the young man and doctor more than himself.

Still, he could not take one more day of this. He was ready to give in. When they dropped him in the cell, he started to crawl to the lone man. He felt himself suddenly lifted from the floor and being carried. He could make out two of the faces of his fellow inmates. Were they taking him to receive his next beating? It turned out that they laid him gently on one of the bunks. The pain kept him awake long enough to realize that his in-house tormentors were no longer around. Next to him sat the only other bunk in the cell and it was occupied by Christian.

"Where are they?" he asked feverishly as if he really cared.

He could not hurt much more.

"They will no longer be able to torment you, my friend," Christian replied softly.

The message did not really sink in. Dustin continued.

"I can't do it anymore, Christian. I don't know how you tolerate it. I tried to have this faith. I just can't do it. Tomorrow I ask for the implant."

"Don't do it, my friend. You are not here to be tried for your faith."

"Then what am I here for."

"You would not understand, at the moment. Just rest, now."

Dustin could not understand much. Especially why the sound of Christian's voice became so soothing. Why his pain seemed to diminish, some. And why his words seemed to put Dustin in a deep, restful sleep.

Dustin woke. *Was he awake*? He heard the muffled sound of gunfire. As if far off from his murky world. He went back to sleep. *Was he asleep*? He was not sure how long he was out, but believed he was woken by a bright light. His eyes blinked rapidly in response to his looking into the light. Out of the light emerged a figure. Then another. As more figures emerged from the swirling mass of light, Dustin closed his eyes. Perhaps this was it. They were coming to get him. Either the tormentors to finish the job. Or—he could not believe that he would ever hope this—perhaps it as God.

CHAPTER NINE

Dustin felt movement. He was rocking back and forth. Occasionally his body tried to leap into the air, but he realized that he was held down with restraints. He could see light coming through many windows and make out people moving about and heard their muffled voices. His mind would not absorb what was going on. So he decided to go back to sleep.

A sharp pain caused his eyes to open. His mind was clearer, and he realized that he was no longer rocking about. He looked around and realized that he was in a large tent. He was still too weak to move much, but he was able to see a little of what was happening to him. His left arm was wrapped. He was covered with a blanket, but could feel wraps around his legs, especially his knees. He reached up with his unhindered hand and touched his head. There were bandages covering various wounds and string in his face. He looked up to see a woman smiling at him. She put the syringe down and patted him on the chest.

She said something, but he could not make it out. She moved on with her tray of implements. She must have given him something and it seemed to be taking effect. He closed his eyes and drifted into a quiet, peaceful sleep.

He opened his eyes again when he felt some kind of tension on his face as he lay on his side.

"Quiet, now," a calm voice spoke. "Don't move."

"What is happening to me?"

A new voice interrupted. A voice he recognized.

"It's all right, Dustin. Just lay still for a few moments longer. They are just removing the last of the stitches," the new voice assured.

"Clarence?"

"Yes, it is me."

"Why did you run off?"

"I didn't *run off*. I went for help. I felt that you would be a drag. I apologize, but you are slowing down in your old age. Now, just lay quietly while they remove the stitches, all right? We will talk later."

At least he knew that he was in a safe place, so he heeded the advice and let the medical technician do his work. He looked into the stomach of the medical person and realized that it was not a he. He moved his eyes so that he could identify the person. It was the woman from the Sheriff's Department in Quinden. At first, it caused him some concern. But then he realized that Clarence was here, so it must be safe. Outside he heard singing. It was an old God song he actually remembered from his youth. What did they call them? *Hymns*? It was the sound of children.

"All right, you are done," the doctor announced breaking his concentration. "If you want to get up, you may. I suggest, though, that you take it slow. Sit up, first, and let your body acclimate. There are crutches beside your bed. Use them for a while. You should be able to walk reasonably well by tomorrow."

"Thanks, Doc."

"I am sorry for the treatment that you received while imprisoned. I did what I could to keep as many as I could alive. I wish I could have done more."

"We all do what we gotta do, Doc. I don't hold a grudge."

"Thanks," she said and moved on to the next patient.

He suddenly realized what he said. He really did not hold a grudge. He was so happy about being alive that there was little room for anger or pity. This God must have pulled him through. But what happened in Quinden?

Dustin took the advice of the doctor and sat up on the edge of—what he now realized was—his cot. His head spun for several minutes. As it began to clear, he saw that he was in a hospital tent with twelve other patients. To his amazement, he recognized the young deputy. Dustin took up his crutches and walked over to him.

"Hey."

"I'm so sorry, man," the deputy said when he saw him.

"Don't worry about it."

"I had to do it. I had to do it to a lot of people. I was hiding out. I didn't take the implant either. It was only a matter of time before they found out. Fortunately, this militia group hit the town hard. Wiped out most of the U.N. troops stationed there. It was an answer to my prayers."

"What's your name?"

"Frank."

"Well, Frank. Learn to forgive yourself. I have all ready forgotten it. Except that mean left hook of yours," Dustin smiled.

The man tried to smile, but Dustin could tell that he was still troubled. Dustin patted his shoulder. He was going to go outside, but he found Christian still dressed in that uncomfortable garb.

"Hey, how are you doing?" Dustin asked.

Christian displayed his legs, both, of which, were in casts.

"They did the best they could. But they feel that I will never walk again."

"Keep the faith. Your God heals, doesn't he? I think I'm starting to get some of that faith."

"That was not why you were tried," Christian reminded him.

"You said that. What was I tried for?"

"What you were tried for, you found."

Dustin thought for a minute.

"Forgiveness?" he said.

"You have only started your spiritual journey, my friend. But it is a good start."

"I didn't start out on no spiritual journey. I'm just trying to stay alive."

"What ever you say. Just keep your heart and your ears open."

"Sure. You might get them to get you some comfortable clothes, though."

"These are mine. It is what I wear."

"Who was that guy that kept coming to the cell when I was being beaten, by the way?"

"It was a man that you met. A man that sought something that you have. He was supposed to take you back. But the Lord stilled his heart for just a moment. To give you time to escape."

"I see," Dustin said not sure if he believed Christian. "What about those prisoners that beat me."

"They were judged and found, well— Lacking."

"Judged. By God?"

"No. By the legal system they served."

Dustin decided not to delve further.

"Well, you take care of yourself. I'll come visit."

"I should like that."

He was about to leave when William entered.

"How are you feeling?" William asked.

"I've been better."

"Good. Because we'll have to move soon. We need to find water." Christian interrupted.

"It will rain soon. Wait ten minutes, and then collect God's water. It will rain for about twenty minutes. That should give you enough time to fill your vessels."

"Thank you, Sir," William responded to him.

Dustin could tell by the tone of William's voice that he expected no miracles. He turned back to Dustin.

"Can we talk?"

"Sure."

The two men went outside and William seemed stunned. Dark clouds were forming in the sky.

"What's wrong?" Dustin asked.

"The clouds have been floating around all day. But nothing like this. Robert!" William called another man over. The man responded. "Get the word out. If it rains, wait ten minutes. Then fill every water container we can find."

"Yes, sir."

"Follow me," William said as the man departed their company.

It began to sprinkle as Dustin followed William. By the time they arrived at a tent, they were wet. Three men waited inside dressed in camouflage. Two of the men stood behind a seated man. The man seated was an older gentleman who still looked like he was in pretty good shape. His head of white, short hair did not detract from his youthful, handsome face. Although the uniforms of the men were void of the standard medallions, their bearing indicated definite military training.

"That's quite a rain out there, Bill," the older man spoke.

"Yes, Sir, it is. Uh, Dustin Conrad, Jackson Palermo."

Dustin nodded.

"These are the men we sought to join. Major Palermo was my company commander in Afghanistan just before the U.S. Forces pulled out. We're Marines. These are the men we were seeking to join."

"I thought that you were an MIT grad," Dustin said.

"I did other things in my idealistic youth."

"How many you got now?"

"Over six-hundred and fifty men. Plus women, wives and children."

"How do you expect to stay hidden with so many people?"

"We move. We dodge. We split. We depend on God. We do what ever it takes to stay hidden. Or we fight."

"Let me get to the point," the Major interrupted bluntly. "We've been able to decipher the information on your flash drive. How did you obtain it?"

"The guy who stole the information helped me out on a few cases. I got it from a friend of his."

"So you know him. He is reliable?"

"I think he is."

"Did he give any information to you concerning who was cloned?"

"No, Sir."

"This is important. Think man."

"The only information I have is on that drive. Just what he downloaded. I assume that it is accurate. The guy *died* for it, after all."

"That is to be expected. Do you realize the implications?"

"Not all of them."

"The world has been on the lookout for what they call 'The Antichrist'. The Bible says, For many deceivers are entered into the world, who confess not that Jesus Christ is come in the flesh. This is a deceiver and an antichrist. We've had antichrists with us since Paul was executed. Napoleon. Hitler. Just about every president and congressman since Woodrow Wilson. All who have tried to destroy the Constitution and drive us into the one world order.

"But they needed one key person to unite them all. This documentation tells us that American Genetics has created the ultimate antichrist. An abomination. The one to unite them.

"I don't know if I particularly believe that man can pull that off, but there in that flash drive they claim evidence that it has been done. If we can link them to any sort of cloning, we might get world opinion on our side. That is why they have been trying to kill you."

"Do you know who it is?" Dustin wondered.

"I have my suspicions."

"Well the only person I know of that is supposedly bringing peace and prosperity back is that U.N. Secretary, guy. Uh, what's his name—Olivi."

"You're very perceptive. You would have made a good cop," the Major said.

Dustin was not sure if the Major knew his history and was just trying to make a joke. He decided to chuckle, just in case. This man was, obviously a powerful leader.

"So, what will you do if you find him? Kill him?"

"That we are not sure of. We need to take it one step at a time. The first step is identifying him."

"How are you going to identify him? Ask that Devlin character?"

"We might not. But reporters just might."

"You won't get a state-controlled reporter to ask that question."

"There are Christian reporters out there. Some are pretty brave. And if Devlin is confronted, he will have to come up with an answer. There might be as much intelligence in what he doesn't say. We are familiar with the concept of disinformation. We used it successfully in Iraq, Afghanistan and Iran when we went in there."

"The rain has stopped," William interrupted the conversation.

"What?" the Major asked.

"The rain. It has stopped. Twenty minutes."

"So what does that mean?" the Major prodded.

"I have no idea, Sir. But that is what that strange one we picked up said."

"Well, if I am no longer needed," Dustin said.

The Major looked at William and William opened the flap to the tent and Dustin departed. He walked around the camp and was astonished at the growth of the army. While he walked, he noticed a man, three boys and two girls come up and inquire about the recruiting method of the militia.

Dustin spotted Clarence sitting by a camp fire. The clouds had moved on leaving its muddy remnant behind, but the sun was setting and it was getting cold, so he decided to join him. He hobbled over on his crutches and sat on the most comfortable rock he could find.

Clarence smiled.

"Thanks for getting me out of that situation in Quinden."

"Don't mention it."

"Are you going to stick around with this group?"

"For a time. You?"

"Well, I can't run very far on my own, at the moment. How do you think they are going to get away with this?"

"With what?"

"You know. How do you think they are going to hide this big of a group from the government's prying eyes."

"The Hebrews did for forty-years, with God's help. And he took them to the promised land."

"Hebrews? You mean, the Jews?"

"No. I mean the Hebrews. Now, the Israelis. Jew is used as a derogatory term, now, so I choose not to use."

"What do you mean they did for forty-years."

"The Exodus. Haven't you ever heard the tale?"

"You mean when they were brought out of Egypt."

"Exactly. Here. It's in here," Clarence handed the Bible to Dustin.

Dustin took the open book into his hands. It was his Bible. Taking it back felt almost as good as a warm handshake from a friend who came to pay him money he was owed. Dustin struggled against the fading light to read the book of Exodus at the point Clarence had opened to. He read quickly so he did not get all of the implications. When he came to Chapter 16, he had questions.

"*Manna*? What is this *manna*?"

"What?" Clarence seemed to snap out of some sort of trance he was in.

"It says here, *And when the dew that lay was gone up, behold, upon the face of the wilderness there lay a small round thing, as small as the hoar frost on the ground. And when the children of Israel saw it, they said one to another, It is manna: for they wist not what it was. And Moses said unto them, This is the bread which the Lord hath given you to eat. Manna. What is it?"

"Exactly."

"Exactly what?"

"*Manna.*"

"Huh?"

Clarence chuckled.

"Sorry. I heard a very old comedy routine by two comedians from the old movies. Abbott and Costello? That was a poor attempt at the Who's On First routine they were so famous for."

"So what is *manna*?"

"It is difficult to explain. It is a food. *Manna* is not exactly the name of the food. It is a question. The Hebrews are basically calling it what is it? Moses explained to them that it is the food that God is providing for them. There was very little else to eat in the desert, you know. And very little water."

"Like here," Dustin commented.

"Oh, this is an oasis compared to their area. Anyway, not only did

God provide shelter and protection as they wandered, he provided them food and the morning dew for water."

"And they called it what is this because they did not know what it was."

"Exactly. You have to remember. The translators of the version of the Bible you read had to translate from ancient Hebrew and Greek texts written by a culture they didn't understand. It's, ah—how do you say it? It loses something in the translation."

"No. It has a certain logic. So it was bread."

"Not really a bread. They used the term bread for food. It was a substance that God provided and hasn't provided since."

"You seem to know an awful lot about this stuff."

"A lot of study, I should say. It is the same principle Jesus uses when he explains that he is the bread of life."

"You mean, *Yoshua*."

"Yes," Clarence smiled. "*Yoshua*. Anyway, he fulfills your spiritual hunger and thirst, if you believe on him, so that you will have everlasting life."

Dustin shook his head.

"I wonder what this *manna* stuff tasted like."

"Tastes like chicken," Clarence replied.

Dustin looked at him and Clarence burst out laughing. Dustin smiled and looked around. He found a small rock that he grabbed and lobbed toward Clarence gently.

"You jerk."

"Sorry. I've been waiting for some time to use that."

After he stopped laughing, Clarence continued.

"Think of it this way. You have a man who spends months, or even years, learning about spices and ingredients. He learns just the proper proportions to mix to make a meal that you are willing to pay big money to taste. How much better from the hand of the being that invented food?"

A man approached with two others. The leader of the group turned out to be Paul. The two men with him carried buckets of water which they dumped on the fire. They used small collapsible shovels to add wet dirt to the mixture.

"Sorry, guys," Jerry explained. "It's lights out. We have to produce a minimal heat signature. You guys should really turn in. We never know when we have to move."

"If you don't mind, I should like to help you stand guard," Clarence volunteered.

"That would be great. Just go over there to the watch tent and he'll give you an assignment."

"I'm still kind of hurting. I'd like to find a bunk," Dustin said.

"That's perfectly understandable. There is a green tent with blue flaps over in that direction. They can get you blankets, possibly a pillow and maybe a cot. But you'd better hurry."

"What about my cot in the hospital?"

"In this environment, when you leave the hospital you are cured. I'm sure that cot is filled by now. And, by the way, I'm glad I didn't kill you."

"Imagine how I must feel," Dustin replied with a laugh.

Paul was apparently not much for humor. He simply turned and walked away.

The stars still dotted the sky and only a sliver of moon reflected the sun to light the landscape. He heard voices, he thought. It sounded like Clarence and Christian talking, but they were speaking gibberish. When he did make out what might be a word, it was undecipherable. That was hardly possible, though, since Christian could not walk. He shook it off and went back to his dream.

Dustin was woken with a start. A militia member was shaking him.

"Get up an pack anything you need. We have to move. There are troops on the way."

Dustin sat up and saw tents coming down quickly. Boxes were being packed into trucks. A couple of trucks were all ready moving with armed escort. Women were scurrying to gather children into busses. Men were taking notes while speaking with the Major. And William was speaking with Christian who lay on his cot. So he was still down. It must have been a dream.

Dustin rose up and used his crutches to help him get over to Christian. His legs were working better, but he still needed a little assistance. As he approached, he started to hear the conversation.

". . .last chance. The other wounded have moved on," William said.

"Just leave me a sharp knife, a couple of those grenades of yours, and a handgun. Perhaps I can cause a diversion to give you time to get away."

"That's very brave of you, and all, but—if I might add— foolhardy. How in blazes do you expect to hold off three-thousand well equipped troops with a couple of grenades and a handgun."

"Leave me one of your machine guns, then. I can take some of them out."

"You are not even going to make a difference in our escape. Now let me get some men—."

"Captain."

Christian interrupted with an interesting word. Dustin never heard William referred to as "Captain." Christian used the term with respect. Indeed, William was a leader of men and had proved himself wise. At least, as far as Dustin was concerned. Christian continued.

"Your own doctors claim that I will never rise again. I will be a burden on you. If you will allow me, I will go out a hero. If only in my own mind."

To the astonishment of Dustin, William pulled three grenades from his bag and laid them beside Christian. He removed his survival knife and laid it with them. Finally, he took out his 9mm and handed it to Christian.

"Those grenades. They are for you, aren't they?"

"What little I know about your troop strengths and movements shall go with me."

"You're not really going to let him do this, are you?" Dustin asked.

"Look. I've got to get this camp packed and moved. I don't have time to argue with a hero. If you can talk some sense into him, fine. I've got things to do."

William left.

"I'm sure he's going to get some guys to get you just before we leave."

"He means exactly what he says. He is a good man. He hasn't gone past his logic, however, to realize that he does believe in God. He'll get there, as you will."

"You have a lot of faith in us, it seems. Just who are you?"

"I have faith in God. And as far as who I am, you can refer to me as Christian."

"But who are you?"

Christian shook his head with a smile.

"Just know this. The rains will follow you. You shall not want for water or sustenance."

"You mean we'll have plenty of bread and water."

Christian laughed.

"I must admit, I hadn't thought of it in your legal terms. That is humorous."

"You've gotta come. I need you."

"What I could do for you, I have all ready done. There is nothing more for me here."

Clarence surprised him with his entrance.

"Hey. Your truck is ready. Let's go."

"We have got to get Christian to come with us."

"Let's go," Clarence said sternly.

Dustin looked around and saw his truck loaded with goods. He looked back to Christian.

"You're welcome," Christian smiled and answered the unstated gratitude.

Dustin went toward the truck. As he did, he heard another statement that Christian made.

"Thank you, Raphael."

They got to the truck.

"How am I supposed to drive?" Dustin asked.

"I will."

Dustin set his crutches in the bed and got into the passenger side. Raphael got into the driver seat. He looked around the steering wheel for a minute.

"Now, let's see. Ah, yes. A key."

He turned the key and the truck started and jerked forward.

"Don't forget the clutch."

"The clutch?" Raphael asked.

"Yes. On the floor on the left."

"Oh, yes. It's clutch. Then the brake. Then the accelerator, correct?"

This time, the truck roared to life without incident.

"Yes. You do have a license, right?"

"Nope. Never driven. But I've been watching you. How hard can it be?"

Dustin laughed heartily. This boy did have a sense of humor. He looked back at the youth as he appeared to be studying the pedals on the floor. He grabbed his seat belt and quickly connected it just in case.

After about a mile, Raphael seemed to have the truck running smoothly.

"Yes. This is rather enjoyable."

"Raphael."

The young man did not answer.

"He called you Raphael, didn't he?"

"Yes, he did."

"Like the painter?"

Raphael's face revealed a bit a relief.

"He was considered an artist, really. But, yes. Just like the painter. Very perceptive of you."

"Just who are you guys, anyway?"

"To whom do you refer?"

"You and Christian."

"Just guys, I expect."

"Turn around."

"What?"

"Turn around. I have the feeling that we are going to need both of you."

"Well, I'm not that important. As for Christian, I do not think that it is a good idea to——." Raphael tried to explain.

"Turn around."

Raphael shrugged and looked for an opening in the convoy.

"You may not like it," he urged.

"Turn around," Dustin persisted.

Raphael turned the truck around and drove back down the road carefully avoiding the other traffic. He got to a point and stopped.

"He told me that you would have to know. He's over there," Raphael pointed.

Dustin got out. He could hear the helicopters in the distance. He might have just enough time to talk some sense into Christian. Dustin started around a bush and saw Christian. He froze behind the bush and observed.

Christian just finished cutting open the second cast with the knife and threw it down. He stood and looked to the sky with his arms stretched. He spoke some words in a language he did not understand, but similar to what he heard last night. Was that *Jewish*? Was he praying to God? He stopped and picked up the 9mm. He looked at it and smiled. He tossed it to the ground beside Dustin causing him to duck behind the bushes.

Had he been seen?

He looked back and Christian turned toward a group of about twenty U.N. troops. They were hollering the standard warnings about getting the arms up and standing still that Dustin had used a hundred times. Christian did raise his arms. He spoke some words and began to glow. A bright, orangish energy, of some sort, jutted from his head and engulfed the troops which were reduced to piles of ash. Wide-eyed, Dustin continued to watch. More troops entered receiving the same fate. A trio of helicopters approached and Christian walked toward them. A wider beam emerged from his head taking them all down in a fiery ball. Christian continued to move toward the oncoming army with the same results.

Dustin was too scared to watch further. He picked up the 9mm and walked, as quickly as he could, back to the truck and got in.

"Let's go."

Raphael started the truck and drove off. As they approached the convoy to re-join, Dustin examined the gun.

"It was as if he tossed this to me. Why?"

"Probably because it seems to comfort you."

"Raphael. If I shoot you, will you die?"

"Please do not test the theory. I'm driving."

Dustin decided not to pursue the subject the rest of the journey.

He quietly thought on the events as the caravan drove down the winding back roads of the wilderness.

CHAPTER TEN

Let no man deceive you by any means: for that day shall not come, except there come a falling away first, and that man of sin be revealed, the son of perdition; Who opposeth and exalteth himself above all that is called God, or that is worshipped; so that he as God sitteth in the temple of God, shewing himself that he is God.—**2 Thessalonians 2:3&4**

ustin woke when the convoy stopped. They located more people. It was dusk, but with enough time to get a few tents up. He tried to help put up a tent, but was politely asked to go and sit down. He was walking, but still not moving as quick as when fully healed. He found Raphael by a campfire and headed toward him. As he approached, he noticed the young woman and the preacher, from the church in Quinden, sitting by the fire. The woman looked grateful while the preacher looked dejected. She was speaking when Dustin approached.

". . .if I had not read Matthew as you instructed, I might have gone. People were calling me on the phone and stopping by my house on the way to the rapture. But I waited. I never went. And the rapture never came."

"I went," the dejected preacher spoke. There were tears in his eyes and a tremble in his Southern drawl. "It was horrible. Like lambs to the slaughter, they came. And me. I was their shepherd. I led them there. I hid and watched as they were . . ."

"You're job was to bring souls to Christ," Raphael explained. "It is their job to read and learn the rules."

"But I led them! I had the only congregation left in Quinden. Half of them are now gone. You think God is going to forgive me for leading so many astray?"

"As I recall in the instruction book, there is only one sin that is unforgivable. Blaspheming the Holy Spirit. You made a mistake. I'm not sure that makes you a blasphemer. Of course, that is God's call, not mine."

"I am responsible for the deaths of over a thousand people."

"I know that you were isolated from what is really happening around the world, so let me explain. Any one that does not have the chip implant is being systematically rounded up for trial or lured into traps. There are not enough prisons. They have ten days to comply or they are executed. People like you kept them from getting the implant through faith. God takes care of his own."

Dustin walked around the fire and stood in front of the man.

"Get a grip, man!" he said angrily. "What he is trying to say is that you made a mistake. It is what you do to correct it that matters. And asking for forgiveness is a part of that." Dustin took out the 9mm and laid it next to the man. "Here. This will be quicker than beating yourself to death."

The preacher looked stunned as Dustin walked away. A confused, Raphael followed.

"Dear fellow. Have you ever thought about a career in the field of psychology?"

"The guy needs to realize that we are all in a bad situation. He needs to get over it and go on."

"Exercise his demons?"

"What ever."

For the first time in a couple of weeks there was nothing to interfere with Dustin's sleep. No voices caused him to wonder. The only pain was that normally felt because of the hardness of the truck bed and the cold of the night. No one jolted him from his slumber to tell him that they had to move.

He dreamed.

For some reason, he dreamed of his mother. Someone he had not thought of for a long time. His father left when he was ten-years old because his mother . . . Well, his mother was a *ding-bat*. She studied all sorts of mysticisms and magic. Any new fad that came along was fair game. It was cool, at first. Halloween every night. Strange things happened in that house, though. Something moved, in that house, that Dustin did not like and it never raised them above the poverty level.

By the time he reached the age of sixteen, he realized none of the mystic tarot cards and potions were of any real use. They never put meat on the table. In his neighborhood, he could go on welfare so that he had extra money for drugs. Or he could raise himself above it and work for what he wanted.

When he turned seventeen, he left his mother, as well. He wasn't even sure if she noticed. He filled out the initial paper work to join the Army, but he never went back. He worked on the docks for awhile. He hated the corruption of the union, but they did get good pay and the benefits were adequate.

He found a circular for college and initially went to a year of law. Realizing that it would take too long to get a law degree, he switched to criminology and got an associates. He could get a job as a cop and take law courses at night. He would, at least, have a steady income. He sometimes regretted not pursuing those law courses.

He actually preferred his initial duty as a cop on the beat. He learned a lot about people from the people. The schedule was fairly consistent and he managed to have an actual life.

Then he got the call that his mother was dying. He went to see her and found a covenant of *Wiccans* dancing around her bed with foul smelling herbs and potions. His mother seemed to just get more and more agitated. After screaming a few choice obscenities, he threw them all out. One of them even left him with a curse. He called a priest to talk to her because he knew they did that sort of thing. They had nothing in common, anymore, so he felt his words would do no good.

After about thirty minutes, the priest emerged from her room and smiled. Dustin went in to find her laying comfortably on her bed and smiling. Her face displayed a calmness that he had never seen in her. She looked at him and spoke with weak, earnest words.

"Thank you, son. Please forgive me."

Then she died. And the sun was in his eyes. His dream had drifted into an awake contemplation. He was not exactly sure how long he had been awake. His thoughts drifted to various times in his life. The bully that picked on him and beat him up in the fifth grade. The time on the docks when he was ordered to hold the coats of three men who beat a "scab" nearly to death. He could have at least called an ambulance. The times that he jumped at the chance to beat a drunk—who resisted arrest by even saying the wrong word—for killing his wife and child. Of all of the things that he did and all of the things that he had done to him, the things that he did seemed to tip the scale against him.

"Yes, mother," he said softly. "I forgive you."

Dustin was growing stronger and able to help collect firewood and water when it rained. He did not eat before the children and the weak and elderly. William took notice of his action and made that a rule. He listened to the daily preaching and prayer, when he could or wanted to. Dustin, also, began to enter the training sessions that the militia held. People were still coming. The area became a small tent city when they arrived. They moved every two to four days to try to prevent their location from being discovered. He continued to read his Bible and was well into the Revelation of Jesus Christ.

Everything seemed to be running smooth, but still his soul was disquieted.

They had just set up camp near the small town of Clarkesdale. A few of the men were sent in to scout the terrain. Dustin and Raphael joined the intelligence gathering mission entering the town. There was very little U.N. troop activity in this area. Only a commander and a small detachment of about a hundred to keep "order." There were prisoners being beaten and yelled at to get the chip. Raphael grabbed Dustin's arm gently and whispered to him.

"Stay still. Now is not the time."

As they passed people, they would see them scratching their hand or forehead and cursing ". . .*those damn Christians*."

Raphael and Dustin entered a bar to duck a few U.N. troops. The bar had no other patrons and was quiet. The bartender stood behind the bar cleaning glasses. His eyes followed them all the way to the bar. The television was turned on to the news channel.

The same reporter was still in Israel. He was somber and Dustin noticed he kept rubbing his hand on his pants as if it itched considerably. The lower third banner told the story.

"U.N. Secretary General shot by Israeli Zionists," it read.

". . .at 11:37 Jerusalem time during the dedication of the temple in Jerusalem. Three Israeli Zionists were arrested in conjunction with the shooting, but it is unclear if they were responsible. Secretary General Olivi was rushed to a hospital where his condition remains unknown.

"Jewish officials would only comment that there was not government involvement in the shooting. They claim that they intend to show documentation, later today, that indicates that the shooters were United States citizens and may not have been Jewish.

"There have been over five-thousand reports, now, of Israeli men disappearing. U.N. officials suspect that Arabs may be rounding them up in response to this latest attack by Israel on the peace treaty. Most Arab officials are denying any responsibility in the disappearances."

"You boys gonna drink?" the bartender asked.

"Don't have any money, sorry," Dustin replied.

"You got a chip?"

"No," Dustin surprised himself with his honesty.

The bartender turned and drew two mugs of beer. He sat them on the table.

"They know you're here," he whispered. "Are you in with that militia crowd?"

"I did not know that there was a militia here," Dustin decided to practice lying.

"Sure. But you tell them that if they are here to free the town, they better hurry. Troops are on the way. It's like they knew you were on the way."

"How do you know all this?"

"I got that damn chip. Before I realized what it meant. But it's kept me alive and in business. Of course, the only business that I have is from U.N. troops. They come in here, get drunk and say things. I act stupid and listen. You tell those boys that if they come in, I have about twenty cases of 9mm ammo and a few UZIs and Desert Eagles stored up."

"What does the chip mean?"

The bartender displayed his right hand. There was a sore forming in the center of his palm.

"It means pain. It's happening all over. Rejection, they call it. Some company is producing a serum that is supposed to stop the rejection. But they are none to quick about distributing it to the plain folk. They were sure faster about punishing people for not getting the chip in the first place. I've watched as they executed a hundred of the town folk. Shipped a lot of them off. I'm sick of these people. I am not old enough to remember when the Supreme Court upheld the Constitution. I'd like to see what a free America looks like."

He turned to Raphael whose gaze was affixed to the television screen. He looked up. It displayed a scene of a massive disturbance in New York. It appeared to center around two men yelling scriptural references and warning people to repent and to turn back to God. One of the men, screaming the warning in the direction of a group of young men, was a tall man with long, grey hair. He had a beard that looked to be about three-weeks in growth. The second man was dressed similar to the first. Dressed in that same garb that he wore in the hospital tent. The second man, issuing similar warnings, was Christian.

"The two men continued to spout warnings and biblical hate message at the crowd who grew around them," the reporter announced. "Riot police had to be brought in to move the crowd in order to arrest the men for hate crimes and disturbing the peace. The two men were booked, but when police went to collect them for arraignment, they were gone. It is not clear how the two men escaped, but citizens are asked to be on the look-out for—."

"Let's go," Raphael interrupted the rest of the news report.

He headed toward the door. Dustin thanked the bartender and followed.

When they got outside, they were confronted by a woman who held her forehead with her hand crying in anguish. She moved her hand and Dustin was shocked to see a portion of the chip sticking out of a hideous sore on her forehead.

By the time the spies returned to the encampment, the sun was setting. Dustin sought William out to tell him what he had learned. He approached and found a couple of the other spies reporting to him as Paul stood by.

"As we were leaving, six *Z-12*s were escorting twelve or thirteen

Hind transports. That's a troop strength of over two hundred men."

"The bartender in town told me that they knew that we were coming," Dustin added.

"What were you doing in a bar?" Paul asked.

"Better that than face the U.N. soldiers that were heading toward us. I did not feel like being recognized. Anyway, he hears things that the troops say. And they seemed to know that we were coming."

"Did he tell you how much troop strength or where they were coming from?"

"No. But he did say he had some cases of 9mm ammo and some weapons at our disposal."

"And you trust a bartender?" Paul asked.

"I told him I didn't have the chip and he didn't turn me in."

"No," William shook his head sadly. "It all makes sense. They herded us here and I fell into the trap."

"Then we should get going," Paul suggested.

"No, Paul, we shouldn't. We can't. There are only two roads in good enough condition for us to travel. They are, no doubt, sending troops down both of those corridors. They waited for us to get into a position where we could not run."

"What do we do?"

"Pray," William suggested. "We pray."

"There is something else," Dustin said. "The Secretary General of the U.N. was apparently shot in an assassination attempt. I don't know what his condition is. You don't suppose that the Major had anything to do with it, do you?"

"I don't know. And I don't really care," William answered. "Sam, Paul. Let's get set up the best we can. Put a squad with grenade launchers along both roads about a mile-and-a-half each way. As the U.N. troops pass, they can open fire. That will alert us that they are coming. And Sam. Tell them the truth. It will probably be a suicide mission. But they will be letting us know that trouble is on the way."

"I'd like to be in one of those squads," Raphael offered.

"Did you just hear me say that it would be suicide?"

"Yes, Sir, I believe I did."

"Well, thanks. Anyway, let's get some holes dug for the children to duck down in and arrange the trucks for protection. Might as well start issuing weapons to the women. We'll need everyone on this one."

"You don't think we're going to get out of this one, do you?" Paul asked.

"I've learned never to ask that, Paul. My feeling right now is that if God wants us to win, he'll have to put a hand in it. Now get going."

The men left and Raphael followed to get instruction. William noticed Dustin standing in place.

"You got something else?"

"Well, I don't know. Christian is alive."

"Christian?"

"The strange guy that was in the hospital tent."

"Oh, yes," William remembered. "The one that wanted to be left behind. How do you know that?"

"I saw him on television. He and another guy got arrested in New York. But somehow they escaped."

"In New York?"

"I didn't want to tell anyone this, because I don't want anyone to think me crazy. But I went back to try to talk him into coming with us. He had cut the casts off of his legs, stood up and some kind of laser beam, or something, came out of his head and destroyed the U.N. troops that were after us that day."

"These have power to shut heaven, that it rain not in the days of their prophecy," William said.

"What?"

"Read Revelation Chapter 11. It's about time that I learned how to pray."

* * *

The doctors worked throughout the night to save Olivi. Devlin observed from the theater. He heard the door open and close, behind him, and the footsteps as some one walked toward him. He was certain that he knew who it was, so he continued to observe the surgery.

"How is he?" Clark asked.

"He had a metal plate in his skull that prevented the bullet from entering the brain. They removed the bullets from his chest and arm. There is no permanent damage," Devlin smiled.

"Where did he get a metal plate from?" Clark wondered.

"A car accident in Geneva," Devlin replied.

"Looks like it saved his life twice. Anyway, I called that number and left the message."

"Thank you, Mr. Clark. You may have the rest of the evening to yourself."

T.O. was curious about the mysterious call. He knew that he gave a code for some nefarious act, but he could not decipher what it could be. And he knew better than to question the Boss.

"Anything else, Mr. Clark?" Devlin continued his interest in the operation.

"No, Sir. Just hope that he's okay."

"Thank you. I'll relay your best wishes."

T.O. turned and left.

* * *

The young priest scurried across the floor of the sanctuary in the Vatican. The Pope needed his medication in a hurry because he had an early day tomorrow and wanted to get some rest. The priest finally reached the door of the Pope's room and knocked. He knew that there would be no answer. He knocked again, waited about fifteen seconds, and then entered. He walked over and set the tray on the desk beside the Pope.

"Your Eminence," he said.

The Pope put all four pills, one at a time, in his mouth. That was his ritual. It was the Pope's way to confirm that he received the right dosages of his evening medications. The Pope flushed the pills down with the six-ounce glass of grapefruit juice.

"Thank you, my son."

The Pope rose and went into his bedroom. The young priest took the tray and left.

It was easy for a young priest to get around Rome without

detection. Only the major Cardinals and Bishops were known by sight. Someday, he would be known by sight. A change of clothes made him indistinguishable from anyone else as he walked down the street with the brown paper bag. He threw the bag into a public trash can and heard the six-ounce glass break when it struck the bottom.

The priest continued to a quieter part of the city and into a side street where a little bar was established about half-way up the block. He entered the tavern which was really a hang out for nearby residents most, of whom, did not concern themselves with religious matters except for the holidays or when a loved one died. He knew no one, and no one knew him.

The young priest looked around and found the blonde man sitting in a darkened corner. He walked over and sat beside him.

"I love Rome," Colbert said. "The coliseum. The fountains. The food, the wine. And the women, whoa."

Colbert looked at the priest.

"Oh. *Sorry*, Father. Hope you don't mind that I ordered you some wine."

"You are forgiven, my Son."

"I presume that you bring me news."

"You are sure the substance is undetectable?"

That answered Colbert's curiosity.

"Colorless, tasteless and odorless. I understand it causes the heart muscle to just seize up. Unless you are specifically looking for it during an autopsy, it is easy to miss," James assured him.

"And me. Will I be *remembered?*"

James smiled and placed his hand on the shoulder of the young priest. He took the hat from the seat beside him with his free hand and covered his blonde hair.

"Your reward is assured, my friend. Now, if you will excuse me, I have to get a new suit."

The young priest watched as Colbert stood and walked out the door. He smiled and drank the wine in two swift gulps. He stood up and went to the door. Now he would be recognized like the Cardinals and the Bishops. He contemplated on his rising fortune, for a moment, and then got up to leave.

He must have risen too quickly and he felt a bit dizzy. He walked to the door and reached for the handle when the pain struck his arm. He was finding it difficult to breath. He realized, in horror, that the pain was shooting across his chest. He looked up at the face of a man who was shaking him and apparently asking if he were all right.

The young priest tried to yell *Treachery!*, but was left gasping for breath.

And the man who stared into his face did not even recognize him.

* * *

"What are you doing in here?" a voice exclaimed.

Devlin and T.O. turned to look. Dr. Richard Ashten stood with them. Dr. Ashten was the practicing physician at *American Genetics*. He was a young idealist recruited right out of medical school by Devlin, himself. His long, dirty-blonde hair lay across his shoulders. There was a constant gleam in his hazel eyes and a smile on his face. He conducted the physicals for all of the employees at the institute. He even found time for physicals for their families. He took special care to be available around all of the sports seasons so that the kids could get their physicals for free. Dr. Ashten took care of Devlin's health, as well. Oddly, Devlin revealed very little about his personal life and Ashten never delved deeper than he needed to. He appreciated being at a research facility where he could learn about the latest advances in medicine. He was just as much in the dark as everyone else about much of what went on inside that facility.

At the doorway, held back by the U.N. guards, was Dr. Goldstein who performed the operation. Dr. Goldstein pushed the guns of the guards aside and forced his way into the room.

"We are visiting," Devlin said.

"Just who the hell are you?"

"I am Dr. Cornelius Devlin."

"Medical doctor?"

"Guilty," Devlin smiled. "But not practicing. Dr. Ashten, here, is a practicing physician and he will take over from here."

"Who the hell gave *that order*?"

"I believe you will find that was a decision between the hospital administrator and the United Nations Security Council. I'm sorry, doctor, my hands are tied," Devlin looked sympathetic. "You will be paid for your services, of course."

"It's not money—."

"You will, certainly, get credit for saving the Secretary's life."

"What is wrong with you? Look, I know you said you don't practice medicine, but I do. I do it because I care about people."

"Of course, Doctor," Devlin said as he nodded to the guards. "I will tell you what I will do. I will ensure that you and Dr. Ashten are allowed to work together."

Goldstein got angrier when the U.N. guards grabbed him by the arms to pull him out.

"I'm going to the administrator," Goldstein threatened.

"Good idea. He will explain everything to you."

Goldstein shook himself loose, turned and left the room. The guards resumed their posts outside the door closing it on their way out. Devlin checked and saw that Dr. Ashten was looking over the chart of the patient and checking the equipment. Devlin whispered to T.O.

"Make sure that the good Doctor gets paid," Mr. Clark.

Clark nodded and left.

Devlin picked up a chair and set it next to the bed of the patient so that he could look into his face. Olivi opened his eyes and looked at Devlin. He smiled.

"Yes, my friend. You are alive. The U.N. has sent us to take care of you."

He pulled Dr. Ashten into view.

"This is Dr. Richard Ashten. He will be responsible for your recovery."

"From what I can tell, Mr. Secretary, I will have little to do with that," Richard added. "You seem to have remarkable recuperative power. However, I will make you as comfortable as possible."

"Thank you, Doctor," Devlin gave him his cue to leave.

Ashten smiled and left.

Devlin looked and read the question in the eyes of Olivi.

"Who? Jewish Zionists, I'm afraid. They had a Jewish doctor

taking care of you, but for security reasons, his involvement has been terminated."

Olivi's expression changed.

"I, also, bring you bad news. The Pope has died of an apparent heart attack. However, we will have a new Pope. A new leader to take us forward. The U.N. Security Council has already drafted a letter to the School of Cardinals outlining who they will recognize as Pope. You can install the President as your successor to ensure the backing of the United States. Best of all, the Board backs you."

Olivi looked quizzical.

"Do not worry, Sir. There were no pious Popes until the 1800s. Before then, they were all Generals and rulers of Rome. We are simply restoring the natural order of the Catholic Church.

"I know this is much to assimilate in your current state of health. Things will seem much clearer in the morning. By tomorrow, you will be up and moving about again."

Devlin smiled as he rose. He took Olivi's hand and watched as he slipped back to sleep. Devlin walked out of the door with a smile.

* * *

A young priest approached Cardinal Bernard and handed him the envelope just as they Cardinals were about to enter the conclave. There would be no messages allowed, thereafter. He smiled for the cameras and was the last to enter the secret meeting. As the door closed, he immediately opened the letter. He cleared his throat and spoke.

"The U.N. informs us that it will recognize only one Pope. One of their own. They suggest that Secretary Olivi be pronounced Pope."

The Cardinals murmured and one rose.

"Yes, Cardinal Martin?" Bernard recognized him.

"This is an outrage, Cardinal Bernard."

"He is a practicing Catholic," Bernard pointed out. "As an added advantage, we will be able to guide the Secretary and the U.N. in making this world much better. We will be able to move our food and medical assistance to where it is need much more rapidly."

Bernard noticed that many of the Cardinals were possibly starting to agree.

"I disagree, I disagree!" Cardinal Martin argued. "What can he know of the inner ceremonies of the Church."

"My friend, Cardinal Martin. We will be able to guide him. We can teach him the ways of the Pope. We've had non-pious popes in the past. The world situation demands that we take charge of this immediately and have a hand in making this a better world."

"If you agree to this, I must resign and oppose you."

Cardinal Bernard sighed.

"You must, of course, follow your heart, my friend. Remember, however, that you have sworn an oath of silence."

Cardinal Martin nodded his head and left.

It cause quite a sensation when Cardinal Martin emerged and left the Vatican without a word. That sensation, however, was quite mild in comparison to the reaction of the crowd outside when the white smoke drifted skyward from the Vatican.

CHAPTER ELEVEN

$\mathcal{P}$reparations continued throughout the next day and into the night. Every twig snap made Dustin nervous. Was it the militia group? Or the intruders? Why were they holding off? Was it to make sure they were into position? Or to make sure that they knew Dustin was the real target?

He began to wish that there was some magical formula in the Bible for faith. Perhaps if he could learn to have faith, it would quiet his soul. He decided that he would prefer not to be taken alive.

This was his first battle. It was quiet. He knew that twelve or thirteen men were placed at the point. They would start the fire fight to alert the main group that the U.N. troops were spotted. Was it always this quiet? The pit for the children was deep enough for all of them to sit down. Trucks had been placed over it and drained of fuel and had all explosive devices removed. They were stuffed with all manner of non-explosives to make them a more efficient barrier against the bullets.

Off in the distance there was a whine. It grew louder quickly and three black Chinese *Z-12* helicopters emerged out of the morning sun. They fired causing glass to burst out of the windows and dust to kick up into the air. The children screamed. Some of the adult did, as well. They fired up at the helicopters in hopes that a lucky bullet might bring one down. As the helicopters swung around, the men in forward positions began firing. The battle began.

A group of men moved forward. They would fire on the oncoming troops so that the forward deployed men could move back to rejoin the main group. If they were alive. The helicopters returned to give another round of fire. This time, men and women went down. Dustin was not sure how many, or how bad. He just fired at the helicopters with the rest.

The explosions expected down the two roads occurred about two minutes apart. Soon the rest of the devastating army would be on them. As the helicopters returned, Dustin noticed that a boy had slipped out of the care of the adults, emerged from the pit and was running across the compound screaming for his mother. It was the boy he saw earlier. Dustin darted across the compound as the helicopters fired again. He grabbed the boy and headed back to the pit. He saw the dirt kick up around him and felt a sting in his shoulder. He fell to the ground, out of breath, realizing he had been hit. He got up and took the boy to the pit and slid him under the trucks. When he saw his face, he realized that the boy looked nothing like his son.

"You stay put, kid."

One of the adults grabbed the boy and sat him down. The shoulder that Dustin was hit in was connected to his shooting arm which was now useless. He rolled over and took his rifle up in his good arm. He fired and watched as the bullets struck one of the *Z-12* helicopters. To the amazement of Dustin, black smoke began to emerge from it. The *Z-12* spun wildly and careened into the ground. He got the lucky shot that they were looking for and a cheer came up from the crowd. Some more men moved forward to assist in taking out the oncoming troops.

Three *Havocs* entered to join the battle. Dustin crawled up to the line to be ready. The other troops should be here any minute. Amazingly, there were still explosions off in the distance in the direction the two groups should be traveling. Were the squads still able to launch grenades? Surely the U.N. troops should have killed them by now.

With a sudden roar, eight more helicopters flew overhead. They did not fire at the militia group. They were not black, but green. They were helicopters that Dustin had seen before. They were army *Comanche* helicopters. They flew past the militia group and engaged the apparently dismayed enemy helicopters. Taking advantage of the surprise, the *Comanche* group destroyed two of the enemy and disabled another. It turned to run, but two went after them.

Dustin looked up when he saw the trucks arriving. They were filled with more troops coming to the aid of the militia. In one of the trucks stood Raphael, apparently ready to report some success down the road.

One of the enemy *Havocs* flew low firing into the truck that Raphael was on. Dustin saw Raphael go down and two missiles flew from the *Havoc*. When the dust settled, the truck was completely destroyed. Men from the other trucks fired hand-held missiles at the *Havoc* which damaged it enough that a *Comanche* could finish the job.

Dustin became angry. He fired a few rounds wildly at the helicopter. He stood and charged recklessly toward the oncoming troops. He gained an element of surprise since they were engaged with the other militia men. He aimed and fired, as best he could, and three or four of them went down immediately. He fired and hit another before they turned on him His weapon ceased to fire as he ran the clip out of ammo. He felt another hit and fell backward onto the ground.

The world became dark.

He woke up in a tent once again. This time he had a mask over his face and a man struggling to keep it on while trying to convince him to remain calm. He looked up and saw a man with a mask
covering his face. His eyes wandered toward his body and he saw a surgeon and a nurse tending to him. He realized that he was in a hospital tent, again, but a much more sophisticated operation. He did calm. He allowed the anaesthetic to do its work and he went back to sleep.

Dustin woke and found himself in a bed. A real bed this time. He looked up at the basketball hoop and scoreboard and was a bit disoriented. He sat up and looked around. He was in a school gymnasium with a lot of beds spread out across the floor.

"Whoa, whoa," he heard a familiar voice.

He looked up to see the Quinden nurse coming toward him.

"Be careful," she warned with a smile. "Your are stitched together with dental floss."

He looked her over carefully. She was attractive the first time that he saw her. But now. . . Now she was beaming. She did not look at worn as she did. Her eyes glowed.

"What?" she asked.

"Well, it seems that if we are going to keep running into each other like this, I should know your name."

"Carole. And if you would quit getting shot and beat up, we won't meet like this," she said.

"Well, then, consider the alternative?"

"Alternative?"

"Yeah. You could go to a movie with me. If they still have one. Or maybe they will hold a victory da—."

The stunned look in her face stopped him. After a second, she had the hint of a tear in her eyes.

"Did I say the wrong thing?"

"It's— It's just that I haven't been invited on a date in quite some time. I don't know what to say."

"If you don't want me to heal slowly from rejection, you could say 'yes'."

She laughed. It was a beautiful laugh.

"Well, I have to admit that is a line I haven't heard used. And I can say— I mean, things may be returning to normal. I can give you a definite maybe."

She giggled and walked away. Dustin smiled and rose slowly. It was chilly in the gym and he could feel the bandages across his side and his right shoulder. His right arm was in a sling, but he could walk. He was a bit tired and dizzy, still, but he had to walk. He walked over to some exercise equipment stuck in a corner where men and women were working out under the guide of a therapeutic nurse. The gym had been converted into a regular hospital.

He looked up and saw William enter with a doctor dressed in a brown uniform and two men dressed in camouflage. The doctor pointed to Dustin and the men walked toward him leaving the doctor to go about his business.

When they arrived, William spoke first.

"Dustin, you have got to chill out," he smiled. "I don't think you have much blood left. Anyway, this is Marine Major Thomas Wilson and Army Sergeant Anthony Jarvis."

Dustin shook hands with each as they were introduced and responded with the appropriate platitudes.

"So God called out the Marines," Dustin commented.

"Well, sort of," Wilson said.

"Major Palermo sent them to check us out," William smiled.

Wilson picked up the explanation.

"We are called the Renegade Squad. We were the first to break away, a couple of years ago, and have been growing ever since. We are a combined force, now. It was just fortunate that the Congress decided to save money years back and allow services to combine duties. We all know how to work together much better now.

"I was sorry to learn about your friend."

The Sergeant added, "We wanted you to know what a brave guy he was. He saved a number of my men. We've been able to monitor enemy transmissions and we knew what was coming. We attacked the groups that were coming down the road. Your friend. It was like he was a trained Ranger. I just wanted you to know that. I didn't know how close you were."

"I didn't either," Dustin shook his head.

Dustin was grieved, but he did not feel alone. A sense of community was starting to restore itself in his life.

"He didn't die in vain," Major Wilson continued. "Right now we have about fifty percent of the rural areas secured in America. If it were not for his actions, we might not have been able to secure this town as a base."

"Do you think that will matter?"

"We're broadcasting news about the war, but we're not sure how many of the city dwellers actually believe it. We need the radio station in this city to cover more area. We're hoping to gain some sympathy, but brainwashing techniques are pretty effective and we still haven't been able to actually hit a major city. But that's our next goal."

"I can tell you from experience that it will be hard to convince the city dwellers without a direct attack."

"Yeah. Especially since Olivi has declared himself Pope," William announced.

"*Pope*?"

"Yes. We found out that he survived the assassination. Apparently, though, it has driven him mad. The Pope died, the other day, and Olivi declared himself Pope. He has, basically, moved the

Vatican into the new temple in Jerusalem. Needless to say, that is a whole other battle.

"But that is nothing to worry about now. You can rest awhile."

"Thanks for the update."

Dustin decided to take the advice and return to his bed. He spotted his Bible, setting on a table by his bedside, next to some medication. He sat, took the pills and laid back to read the book of Revelation.

He suddenly shot up. He was finding it difficult to breath. He frantically waved an arm around and fell to the floor. He felt himself being lifted up and arms wrap around his chest. He felt a squeeze on his chest and the pill that was caught in his throat shot out of his mouth. Dustin looked around through teary eyes at the medical staff around him.

"You all right?" the doctor asked.

He grabbed the glass of water from the nurse as he nodded his head and gulped it.

"Yeah. Thanks."

"No problem. Just ask for water next time."

Dustin woke up rested the next day. Doctors examined him and were amazed at his progress. Tomorrow they would remove the stitches. He walked outside and sat. It was cool, but the sun was out warming the earth. It should have been much colder. The birds were singing and people were walking about laughing and talking. The children were playing. It had a feel of normalcy. He began to read his Bible, but was soon interrupted by a female voice.

"I wanted to thank you, Mr. Conrad. For saving my son."

He looked up into the eyes of the mother of the boy he saved. He started to stand.

"Don't get up. I did not really want to disturb you."

"It's Dustin. And it was nothing."

"It was everything to me. I just wanted you to know how much I appreciated it."

"Well, you're welcome," was all he could think to say.

"If you'd like to meet him, we are going to have a little get together tomorrow. Real food," she smiled.

"That's an invite I cannot refuse."

Dustin went back into the hospital to press Carole for that date. Now they had someplace to go. Surprisingly, she accepted.

The next day he was nervous. He had not been out on a date in some time. His only consolation was that Carole hadn't either. And he thought the dating scene was murder just a few months ago. After his sponge bath, he went into the restroom and continued to clean where it did not hurt too much. That was precious little area of his body. A giggling doctor managed to create a cologne, for him, that did not stink too bad. Candy and flowers were out, so he decide to just go to the address that Carole gave to pick her up. He was late getting there between finding the address and the minor aches and pains associated with having not been able to walk for a length of time.

He knocked on the door of the house which had been turned into a single ladies dormitory. When the door opened, he was taken aback. She was beautiful. She was dressed in an elegant gown and they had managed to scrape up some make-up—not that she used, or needed, a large amount.

"Are you ready to go?" he asked nervously.

He heard the giggling and followed her eyes to some girls who stood in the living room of the dormitory.

"Don't worry. I've been getting that all day."

"Man, you need to get a television."

She looked at him and smiled. They left for the dinner party. As they walked and the sun set, Dustin noticed a smile on Carole's face.

"I'd give you a penny for your thoughts, but I don't have any credit on my chip," Dustin said.

Carole laughed.

"Sorry. I was just thinking, you know—. Well, I was just thinking how nice this is. It almost seems normal. Like it used to."

"Well, we still have a long way to go."

"I know. But it's nice."

"How did you get wrapped up with that sheriff's station in Quinden?"

"It was a one-thing-led-to-another type situation. They were bugging me about getting the chip. They killed most of the medical people in the town for refusing to get the implant.

"Joe Thompson was the Sheriff's second in command. Well, he was the Sheriff, in reality. The sheriff is a drunk and had been out of the picture for a year, or so. He couldn't handle the changes. Thompson grew up the town bully and it just continued. He needed someone to keep people alive long to endure his torture and he had a thing for me.

"Anyway, I was kind of volunteered. It helped me delay getting the chip because I was always too busy keeping you guys alive. Anyway. . ."

Her voice trailed and Dustin could tell it was a sore subject.

"I get the picture."

"What about you?"

"Well, my wife and son died in a car crash about two-years ago. I was a cop. I always felt like I should have been on duty, or something. I couldn't save them. I wasn't there. I blamed everyone else, outwardly, but inside I guess I felt like I should have been able to stop it. I was helpless."

"That wasn't your fault."

"I know that now. But if I had learned that earlier, I might have gotten remarried. Had three-point-five kids and settled down. Who knows, I might have even gotten the chip. But then I wouldn't have met you."

"That's sweet," she said and reached over and gave him a kiss on the cheek.

Dustin stopped and stood in front of her.

"You shouldn't have done that," he said.

"Why not?" she smiled.

With his good arm, he pulled her head toward his. He closed his eyes as his lips met hers. They kissed and kissed again. When their heads separated, he could see that it had the desired effect.

"Come on. We're all ready late," he smiled.

"And I haven't eaten all day. I'm hungry," she commented.

They rang the bell and the mother answered the door. He didn't know her name, so he waited for her to introduce herself as Ruth. They entered. Dustin immediately noticed William and Major Wilson talking. Paul and Sergeant Jarvis stood near by chatting. Everybody spoke politely to one another, but said very little. No one wanted to bring up the darkness that hung over the world. For tonight, this was the world. Every one spoke about good old times as if they happened yesterday without the interdiction of the evil they now lived under. Dustin knew, though, that everyone was still nervous about tomorrow.

Ruth brought the young boy to Dustin.

"David, this is Mr. Conrad. He's the man who saved you."

"Sorry you got shot, Mr. Conrad. My mother was in danger."

"Well, David, it seems pretty clear that she can take care of herself. You need to keep your head down."

"I wasn't going to get hurt."

"Why not?"

"God protects me."

Dustin knelt.

"I hear that's true," he smiled. "But he doesn't put up a magic shield to protect us from bullets in flight. I'm a living testament to that fact, my friend."

"But you are alive," the boy reminded him.

Dustin was stunned. Did this kid just say that? Was it a childlike observation or a message? Was it borne from his heart or from some other source? He was alive. The bullets could have hit a major organ. He did the same thing that the boy did when he saw Raphael killed, after all. Whatever the source, the statement certainly had an impact.

"Yeah, kid. I guess you are right. But you take care of yourself, okay? Keep your head down."

"Yes, sir."

Dustin rose slowly and watched at the boy walked away.

"I hope he wasn't being impertinent," Ruth said.

"From the mouth of babes," he said.

The meal was marvelous. They had roast beef, potatoes, a salad and wine. Of course, everything was rationed to ensure everyone ate. Dustin ate slowly to make it last. He was actually full and not able to complete the meal with the scheduled desert of apple pie. With real apples.

They said their good nights and Dustin walked Carole home under the clear, starry sky. There were only necessary lights burning and some were flickering indicating that they required maintenance. The full moon did most of the lighting. Dustin paused about half-way back to the dormitory. He looked in her eyes and kissed her again. He wanted to see if he were dreaming the kiss before. This time, her return kiss was more enjoyable; more intense. He did not even feel this way toward his deceased mate. It seemed all too surreal.

"I just thought I'd get that out of the way now. To avoid the giggling crowds," he said as he stroked her soft hair.

She hugged his hand.

"I mean, there are rules. I don't suppose I can go in."

"Nope. We're living the Christian lifestyle, now."

"Well, it isn't so bad," he replied. "I think I'd change a couple of rules. But then, I'm not God, am I."

"No. But you make me feel good."

"I'd like to see you again."

"I'm not going any where," Carole laughed.

He wrapped his good arm around her waist and escorted her the rest of the way home. He watched her as she walked to the dormitory door and knocked. The porch light came on. The door opened and a blonde stuck her head out and grinned. He nervously waved a good bye.

Dustin had to pass through the downtown area to get back to the gymnasium. He never felt safe, even as an armed cop, walking through the darkened city streets. He liked this new, small-town feel. He danced down the street despite his aches. He paused when he saw something in the store window. It was his reflection. He smiled. He pressed his face against the window and discovered it was a clothing store. There was a rather nice suit on a mannequin inside. He never owned a suit. He might have to stop by tomorrow and see how much it costs.

He drew his head back to smile at his reflection once more. His smile quickly faded. There was *another* reflection in the window beside his. A face he never expected, nor wanted, to see again. There was a sudden, sharp pain in the back of his head and he blacked out.

CHAPTER TWELVE

*D*ustin found himself waking up after injuries entirely too many times. He looked down and found that he was quite securely bound with rope. This time he was not held down by restraints and felt every bump and jolt. He looked up and saw T.O. smiling down at him.

"Well. We're awake."

"How long have I been out?"

"Only about fifteen minutes. You might as well go back to sleep. It is a long journey. The Boss is anxiously awaiting your arrival."

"And who is the Boss?"

"That would be Cornelius Devlin."

"You know, that guy is really a jerk. You guys ever thought of forming a union?"

"Shut that fool up," Dustin heard the disembodied voice.

"Who is that?"

"That would be your driver. I recommend being quiet and going back to sleep. It would be better for you that way."

"How do you expect to get through our gauntlet without getting stopped."

"Why this is free America," T.O. laughed. "We can come and go as we please."

* * *

As it turned out, it was a long trip. It was the bumping around that made it a long trip; not so-much the distance. Dustin slept as much as he could. He felt that he would probably need to be rested up. The van suddenly stopped bouncing around, so Dustin assumed they had finally reached paved roads. Except for the occasional pothole, the trip was smooth the rest of the way.

He had all ready guessed that their journey would end up at *American Genetics Laboratory*. He felt the van drop down, so he surmised that they were going down into a lower garage area. When they finally pulled him from the van, he found that he was right on both accounts. They dragged him up to face Devlin.

"Lieutenant Conrad. You don't know how long I've been waiting for you."

"Almost three months, hasn't it been?"

Devlin slugged him in the gut. Devlin was not a big man and certainly looked the part of the geeky scientist. But he did pack a punch.

"Take him," Devlin ordered.

The men took Conrad into a large room. He was not shown this room during the investigation and he realized why. It held a collection of torture devices used throughout the centuries. They stripped him down to his underwear not being too careful about keeping his clothes in tact. He feared that they felt he would no longer require clothes.

They laid him on a table and strapped him down as his wounds began to ache. They placed his head in a brace that allowed for no movement. They dragged something over and placed it over his head. He could see some kind of adjustment screw. T.O. turned it and something shot out toward him and hit him in the forehead. It was cool and ran down the side of his head. Another drop hit his forehead about a minute later.

Water?

Right again. Every minute, he felt a drop hit his forehead. T.O. smiled and walked away.

Count the drops.

The lights extinguished leaving him in total darkness.

* * *

T.O. was following Devlin to his office. Along the way, Devlin had to stop in a chamber that T.O. had never entered. Devlin did not seem to mind that T.O. entered right behind him. T.O. paused next to a tube while Devlin walked across the room to an electronic console and began tapping at a computer keyboard. T.O. glanced at the tube and looked around. He saw that the room was filled with these tubes. Thirty, or more, it appeared. The tubes were seven or eight-feet in length and about four-feet in breadth. Each were connected to all manner of wires and tubes and had a small window in them. He set his hand on one and drew it back quickly. They were cold. He looked up to see that Devlin was still engrossed in his work. He moved up to the window of the nearest tube and wiped the frost from the glass. He looked in and jumped back with a start. Inside the tube, a swirling mix of gas floated about. On this occasion, it swirled around and cleared up enough so that Clark could see that he was staring at the face of Olivi. Did Devlin clone Olivi? Did all of these tubes contain a replica of the new Pope? Clark remembered back to the tour Olivi took of the facility. Did Devlin intend to use these clones to keep Olivi alive indefinitely? Had he all ready used one?

Another thought suddenly struck Clark. What if Olivi, himself, was a clone? Whom was he a clone of? In that event, what would all of these replicas possibly be used for?

* * *

Drip. Drip. Drip.

If he could count the drops, he would know how long he had been there. He heard of this. The water torture. He had to keep his head.

Drip. Drip. Drip.

Thirty-eight. . .thirty-nine. . . Wait. Did that drop hit him in a minute or thirty seconds? Just count. What was that? Oh, yeah. Forty. . .forty-one. No. It was fifty-eight. Oh, damn. Another drop went into his eye. Fifty-eight. . . No wait, forty-one.

The monotony was broken when a dim light came on and he received a visit from Devlin.

"Hey, there, Sport. How are you feeling?" Devlin smiled.

"I need to go to the bathroom, Sport."

"Well, go. Who is stopping you."

"You're an ass."

Devlin laughed.

"Oh, the impertinence. It's kind of a welcome relief, you know. So many *Yes* men around me all the time."

"How long do you intend to keep this up?"

"This. Torture is a little hobby of mine. An aside, if you will, to break up the monotony of the daily routine. I like to test the water—pun intended—and see how much a man can endure.

"This is something I've always wanted to try. The water torture. And I thought that we should start out with something light, with you being hurt, and all. It should last. . . Oh— Until I break you," his tone turned dark. He calmed and smiled again. "Shall I tell you how long you have been here? Or have you guessed?"

"How long."

"I'm sorry. I'm not allowed to tell you. That is all part of the game, you see."

"I see. You know, I don't have the drive anymore. The information is all ready out there."

"The drive and the information is no longer of consequence. It doesn't matter to me any longer, don't you worry yourself about that."

"Then why?"

Devlin's demeanor changed instantly.

"Because you have been a boil on my butt since this whole nasty affair began! And do you know what we do with boils?"

"We let them fester until they give up and finally go away?"

"We lance them, Lieutenant Conrad. We lance them. As I shall lance you until I pierce your heart. Into your very soul. Until I break you, Lieutenant Conrad."

"If you don't mind, could you call me Dustin? I don't think I'm a lieutenant anymore."

Devlin laughed.

"Yes, Dustin, sure. This might be a more enjoyable experience than I imagined. If I can break you, well— I might be able to break just about anybody." Devlin patted him on the arm. "You get some rest now."

Devlin laughed as he walked away. The lights went out once more.

Drip. Drip. Drip.

The only interruption in this damnable schedule of dripping was the visit to give him a drink of water. Of water. The very taste of it was becoming bitter in his mouth. No food. Not a morsel of bread. Just water.

How long would this go on? Think. Maybe the scripture. What was the advise of Paul the Apostle? Finally, brethren, whatsoever things are true, whatsoever things are honest, whatsoever things are just, whatsoever things are pure, whatsoever things are lovely, whatsoever things are of good report; if there be any virtue, and if there be any praise, think on these things.

* * *

Dustin drove into the parking lot of the hospital as carefully as he could, considering that he was speeding. He found a parking space and turned the revolving patrol-car lights off. He leapt from the car and brushed off his black uniform as he darted for the door of the hospital. His uniform was not dirty. It just became a habit with him. Next week he would trade in his Sergeant stripes for bars. Right now, he had a week off to take care of business.

He went into the waiting room of expectant fathers. He looked through the glass frantically searching for his off-spring. Dr. Benjamin entered and took him by the arm.

"How is she, Doc? Where's my baby? Sorry I couldn't get here."

"Listen. Calm down, all right?" Dr. Benjamin spoke in a calm, but controlling voice. "Now there was a little problem that you should be aware of. The baby and your wife are fine, you got it?

It's just that you may not have anymore children."

"Why? What happened?"

"I'll explain it to you and Darla later. I just wanted to let you know up front. But you have a fine baby—."

"*What*? Baby *what*?"

Dr. Benjamin smiled.

"You have a fine baby boy."

"Fine? What do you mean fine? All his toes, all his fingers. That sort of thing."

"He's perfectly healthy. And your wife is in good condition."

"Where are they? I mean, can I see them?"

"Follow me."

The two men walked down a hall to the room where his wife lay on the bed.

"Private room? This is gonna cost me a fortune."

"It's not a private room. It was just unoccupied, at the moment. Don't worry Dustin. I have seniority. You remember who else I delivered."

"Yeah. You may regret that if you ever run through a red light."

"And after I was going to fudge the accounts," Doctor Benjamin laughed.

Dustin went to the side of his wife's bed. He looked her in the eyes. Her bright, brown eyes. The eyes that caused him to be attracted to her in the first place. He clasped his hands and put them against his mouth as he tried to hold back the tears.

"You're beautiful, baby," he said.

He *did* love her. He loved here very much. From the time he met her and stared into those beautiful eyes, he loved her. He loved her through the times that they subsisted on cans of pork and beans, jars of peanut butter and packages of Ramen noodles. And he loved her now more than ever.

"You want to meet your son?" she smiled.

"What? Oh, is this for me?" he smiled.

He lifted his son into his arms. He looked into his beautiful, bright eyes. His son smiled up at him.

"Hi. I'm your daddy. I'm the one who is going to give you all those whippings. What do we call him?"

"I thought about George."

"That's my dad's name," he replied softly and sadly not taking his eyes from his infant son.

"We can call him something else. We have time to think of a name."

"Not much. He's all ready got a social security number. Hey, maybe we could just use that," he smiled.

Dustin reached down and kissed his wife. He rose up and looked into the face of his baby boy once again.

"He's got your eyes, you know. Of course, he's got my, well— You know. But he's got your eyes definitely."

"I know, I know," Darla laughed.

It didn't bother Dustin to be woken up, in the middle of the night, by the cries of the hungry baby. He rather enjoyed it. With his new work load, it was these short periods of time that he could spend with his son that were so precious. He lifted the child from the crib and stuck the nipple of the bottle in his mouth. He sat down and watched his son eat.

"You know boy, you are a gift from God," he told the boy who looked up at him and smiled between sucks. "So what are you going to be? A football star? A rock star? Perhaps an opera singer. An actor. Anything but a cop, okay? You come home and say that you want to be a cop I'll beat you senseless."

The baby boy laughed. Dustin looked up and in the dim light saw Darla standing there. She smiled and mouthed I love you.

He mouthed I love you, too in return.

Dustin sat reading the paper in the dimly lit room using the light from the lamp that stood next to his chair. He was skimming the newspaper, really. It was all the same old stuff. The baby was quiet. He was listening to an oldies station on the radio. There was a soft rock tune by *The Hollies* playing. He looked up and saw Darla standing there. She seemed to shine even in the dark. He let the paper slip down as he went to her and took her hands in his. He drew her close and put an arm around her waist as the tune wafted through the air. *All that I need is the air that I breath and to love you.* They danced.

It was one of those lazy weekends. They went out by the lake for their picnic. Another week off was about the end. He found the tire swing hanging from the tree by the lake.

"Stay off of that swing!" Darla warned. "You don't know how long that has been hanging there."

"It's been there since I was a kid and it's been fine. I know what I'm doing! Take notes, kid. You're next," he told his son.

He went next to the tree and gave a Tarzan yell. He stepped into the swing and stood holding the rope for support. He swung out over the lake and waited for the tire to return the other way. He pushed and the swing went further over the lake. It was great. He felt like he could get the swing to wrap around the limb that held the rope firm. So he pushed harder.

That is when things went terribly wrong.

He found himself flying feet first, tire and all, over the lake. He hit the water with a splash and sank underneath.

Water!

He rose up and came out of the lake holding his back. His wife looked worried, at first, but then burst out in laughter.

"You would laugh at a broken man?" he sneered as he lay down on the blanket beside her.

Darla laid on top of him.

"You're not broken," she smiled. "You're unbreakable."

She kissed him. Long and hard. It was horrible. Her spittle ran down into her mouth. It was bitter and he spit it out.

* * *

Was he screaming?

Some men lifted him up and threw him on the floor. He heard Devlin's muffled voice.

"You still with us?"

He felt some slaps across his face.

"Come on man. Beg me for your life. Come on. Say something."

"I could use a shower," Dustin replied.

"Did he just say that? Is he tough, or what? Put him up," Devlin laughed.

A tingling sensation woke him. He was hanging with his arms and legs spread apart. There was another tingle. A shock. He yelped. He looked up at Devlin who grinned at him.

"Pretty cool, huh? This is another experiment, you see. The chains that bind you are electrified. Don't worry. It's only direct current. Do you understand what that means?"

"Not really."

Dustin yelped as another shock went through the chains.

"No matter. What matters is that you will receive a periodic jolt. The current and the intervals shift. That way, you never know when or what to expect. Sometimes, you will receive a tiny shock. Just to let you know that you are alive. At other times—."

Dustin screamed as he received a larger dose of current.

"Oh, yes. Big jolts. Now, I should explain that down by your left foot is a button. If you can reach it and press it, it will sound an alarm and I will come running with the chip. You will take the implant and be free to enjoy the rest of your life. May even be a fat paycheck in it for you. You might be able to replace that wife of yours. What is her name? Darla?"

"Shut your mouth you filthy pig. Don't you ever mention her name."

Devlin produced a long needle.

"You ever have a voodoo doll? Tell me what this feels like?"

Devlin proceeded to drive the needle slowly into Dustin's ribs. As he did, another jolt hit. Devlin jumped back waving his hand and sending the needle flying into the air with a smile.

"Wow. I didn't expect that one. You take care, now. And don't disappoint me, okay. The button is right there."

"A friend of mine once told me, *Fear none of those things which thou shalt suffer: behold, the devil shall cast some of you into prison, that ye may be tried; and ye shall have tribulation ten days: be thou faithful unto death, and I will give thee a crown of life.*"

Devlin screamed and took the chance of hitting Dustin across the face.

"Do not spout Jesus quotes to me! There are people dying out there, Dustin. Dying because they won't accept a simple, necessary requirement to keep order and discipline. You can change that. Simply lead by example and take the chip and we'll all be much happier.

"You know, my friend. We are a lot alike. I grew up with a Christian mother who loved me. A mother who took me to Church and taught me love. Yet, I know that this new god will reign supreme and bring final peace on the earth."

Dustin snickered. Then he began to laugh at the absolute absurdity of what he had just heard.

"What?" Devlin demanded as his demeanor rapidly shifted.

"Boy, you have a lousy researcher," Dustin burst into laughter.

"Stop it!"

Devlin moved to a rack and pulled an object from it. He went back and bludgeoned Dustin across the head until he could contain his laughter. He had to admit, internally, some satisfaction at getting Devlin worked up. Apparently Devlin could not stand to be laughed at.

But it was a painful strike. Dustin recognized the instrument. The police used it as part of the non-lethal means of subduing a suspect. It was a club made of hard, flexible rubber that did not damage anything, but definitely got your attention.

Dustin yelped as he was hit with another shock.

"All right, all right. If you are going to be difficult. I'll leave you alone to think on it."

Devlin left.

Dustin remembered what the Major said about intelligence. Sometimes, what was left unsaid the most important. He remembered what Devlin had done to the girlfriend of Anthony. Devlin had not mentioned Carole. The chances were that he knew nothing about her. That gave him a little more strength to resist.

Dustin noticed, over time, that the lights flickered ever so slightly just before he received a jolt. He had a means to prepare for the jolts, now, but he was not sure if it mattered.

The light flickered.

* * *

The street light flickered, he noticed, as he looked at the starry sky. Carole and he held hands and walked through the street lit mainly by the light of the full moon. There was a twinkle in her eyes. Part of it seemed to be a reflection of the moonlight. He still could not believe that he asked her out. He could not, quite, believe that she accepted. Yet, here they were. He moved his lips to hers and they kissed.

He admitted it to himself. Someday he would have to get around to asking her to marry him.

* * *

The lights flickered and he received another jolt. How long this time? This was getting old. He became numb to the pain. His body jolted, now, simply as an involuntary reaction to the current.

He felt himself fall to the floor. His mind was numbing. He could see something on the floor. *Manna*? It was bread. He bit into it. He could barely see the bugs crawling on it. He took another bite.

"Dude's hungry," he heard a voice.

Then he consumed the remainder. In his mind, it came from the God who invented food.

Dustin woke up in a cell. How long had he been out? Was his ten days up? Was this the final day? The door opened and a couple of goons blocked the exit.

"Good. We don't have to wake you," one of them said.

He, and the other man, grabbed Dustin and pulled him out of the cell. They escorted him back to the torture room. Devlin sat sipping tea at a table. He seemed discontent which pleased Dustin. Devlin nodded and his assistants brought a pitcher of water from which Dustin was allowed to drink his fill.

"Dustin, I must admit. You are a worthy adversary. I'm beginning to believe that you will not break. But that is not possible, is it? I mean, every man has a breaking point, doesn't he?"

Dustin shrugged meekly.

"Your friend, Dwayne, broke down by this point. Begged me for the chip. I gave it to him, of course, after he begged enough. He's back on the force enjoying life with his loving family.

"Do you have a breaking point? Let's find out."

Devlin picked up a remote device and pressed a button. A four-foot by four-foot portion of the floor opened up in a corner of the room. Dustin was pushed into the corner and let out a scream. He looked down to see the spikes that were causing the pain. A cage came down around him that fit exactly around the four-by-four area of spikes.

"Now this one is a variation of a theme used effectively in Viet Nam. You will have to stand there until you can stand no longer. Eventually, you will have to kneel or sit down, or something. Just imagine the intense pain that will cause."

Dustin leapt to the bars and grabbed hold. The bars were spaced just far enough apart that he could grab them, but he could not get his feet through. He was able to hang on to the edge with his toes and hold the bars so that he was off of the spikes.

"Hey, hey," Devlin said with glee.

He stood and walked toward the cage.

"You've just added a dimension that I had not thought of. Well, 'All's fair in love and war', I've heard it said. The question remains, though, just how long can you hang on. I mean that literally, of course."

Devlin started pulling on the fingers of Dustin's right hand and Dustin responded by moving it to another bar. Devlin laughed.

"I'm just kidding. I'm not going to disturb your little ruse. I like a man with spirit. You'd do well on my team. Of course, to join you only have to do one thing. One little thing. Take the chip and love Pope Olivi as we all do. As I do."

Devlin paused for an answer. Dustin just returned a defiant gaze.

"Very well, then. I have some things to attend to, but I will try to get back in an hour, or so, to see how you are doing. I hope you realize what I am doing for you. Those barbaric U.N. troops use simple beatings to try to get people to take the chip. I am giving you a challenge. See you later.

"I almost forgot. Before I go I wanted to leave you with a little entertainment."

One of the goons wheeled a large, flat-screened television into Dustin's view. He turned it on with a remote and Dustin saw Olivi walking the streets of New York in full Pope regalia blessing people. Dustin personally had little use for a Pontiff. Even he, though, found this abomination disgusting.

"I take it that you only have basic cable. No football games on?" Dustin commented.

"Just watch. Maybe witnessing the power of Olivi will help you think."

Devlin and the others left. Dustin tried not to watch. He did not want to watch. How long could he hold on? If Dwayne really did turn, how long could he possibly hold on? The voice of the announcer drew his attention to the screen.

"This video was taken by a New Yorker where Pope Olivi is blessing the citizens," the newscaster reported. "Yet, this video shows Pope Olivi in Paris. And yet another from Hamburg, Germany. A hundred sightings are reported around the world. In Ethiopia. Mexico. Canada. Even the tiny island of Cuba reports that Olivi is there performing miracles.

"At the same time, our reporter in Jerusalem has a report on Pope Olivi. Jerry?"

The scene switched to the new temple in Jerusalem. Thousands of people stood outside as the Pope of the Holy Roman Empire emerged from the Temple of Jerusalem to give his blessings. The lower third indicated that this was a live report.

"That's right. As you can see, thousands of people have flooded the temple mount to receive the blessing of His Eminence, the Pope. It's a feeling that I cannot describe. Even though I've had a rejection problem with the chip," the reporter held up his hand to display the sore for effect, "I, like so many here, are praying to Pope Olivi that he will heal us as he has so many around the world. His appearance around the globe only shows how great his power is."

How could that be? There was only one Olivi, right? He could not possibly have that power. The crowd cheered as Olivi emerged. The raiment he wore was strange. Much different than the Pope. The gold on it glittered. It was real gold. He did not wear the mitre that people had become accustomed to. The wore the Triregnum. It was a gold, jewel-encrusted three-tiered crown. In his hand was a scepter which appeared to be made of ivory with rubies fashioned in the shape of a dove on the end of it.

He started to speak and the crowd quieted. He spoke some words, that Dustin guessed were Latin, for about three-minutes. He then started speaking in English.

"Blessings to you, my children. I have brought to the world peace. My blessings shall ever be upon you, now. I am your king. There will be no more corruption. All will be fed. All that follow me will know peace and love. The *Hebrews* wanted a king like the other nations. Now the nations all have one king! The nations all have one loving god! The nations all have one humanity!"

The crowd went crazy with cheering. The camera turned to what appeared to be a disturbance. An orange glow and screaming caught Dustin's eye. Two men came into view and walked up to the Pontiff. They were dressed in the sackcloth which had become their trademark. It was comforting to see Christian once again.

"The Hebrews wanted a king like the other nations, and they learned the sorrow. This is an abomination which stands before you!" the other man said.

"I have brought you peace. Can your god do so?"

"You have brought the image of peace," Christian argued. "Every evening on your State-controlled, corporation paid media you bring images of peace. In your large, army-controlled cities you have brought the illusion of peace. But there is not peace. No peace for the lambs you have slaughtered for not getting your identification mark. No peace for the rebel souls which march against you even as we speak!"

The other man took up the gauntlet.

"My God has proved himself to Jezebel with fire. Can you prove yourself with water? Make it rain. Pray to your god, people. Pray he make it rain. If I set this crowd ablaze, abomination, can you save them with water?"

"*Be thou faithful unto death, and I will give thee a crown of life, saith the Lord!*" Christian shouted.

Did Christian just say that? Or was it the imaginings of a man gone mad? Dustin's hands were sweating and slipped on the bars. How much longer could he hold on?

The crowd began chanting Kill them! Kill them! Bring us peace!

The television briefly went dark. It lit, once again, with a commercial. A scene of a concert hall with an orchestra playing peaceful, restful classical music interjected with a dose of electronic mix.

"The Concert for the Pontiff featuring this age artist Murdoch Hamm. Tonight at 8 over all of these glorious channels," a voice-over announced.

The television abruptly shut off and one of Devlin's goons dragged it away. Dustin assumed that they witnessed the account and tried to get the television out of the room before Dustin received any encouragement. It was too late. Was it too little, however? Dustin held on. He was not sure how long he could hold on to the bars. He was not sure how much longer he could hold on to his sanity.

Dustin stepped down into the pit. He screamed in anguish as the spikes opened new wounds. He knelt down and instinctively laid his hand out to prevent himself from falling forward. He pulled his hand up and cried.

"I don't know how to do this, God. I've never done this. *I do not know how to ask you, God, to save me.*"

Despite the pain, he tried to sleep and was successful.

The cage lifted up rousing Dustin from his sleep. He was close enough to the side that the goons could retrieve him without a problem. He was carried on a gurney to a room where a man waited. The man gently tended to his wounds. While Dustin was grateful, he realized that this man was no Carole. The man finished and the goons wheeled him into a hall way and they moved down the corridor. He looked up as the lights passed overhead. It was a similar feeling to that he had when he was shot, as a cop, and being wheeled through the hospital as he desperately clung to a thin thread of life.

They stopped moving and he heard a door open. The men lifted Dustin from the gurney and carried him into a room. They stood him so that they could put a soft, white robe on him and tie it shut. They laid him on a bed and covered him with a blanket. When they left, they closed the door and Dustin heard the sound of a lock being engaged.

"Well, I'm still a prisoner," he thought.

But what was happening? Were they resting him up for the next round? He was weak, but he looked over at the night stand and saw the pitcher of water. He sat up and spilled some of the water into the glass next to it. It looked like water. It poured like water. He sipped it. It was wet and tasted like fresh water. It had the same quenching effect. If there was anything wrong with it, he guessed that he would soon learn. He drank the rest of the glass and wiped the excess from his lips. Dustin sat the glass down. He laid back down and slipped into a deep, restful sleep.

Dustin woke. He sat up and took notice of the size of the room. It was rather large, for a prison cell. In the center of the room was a table onto which a silver setting had been placed. He stood up and walked over to it. He pulled off the lid from the larger plate and found a steak with baked potatoes and green beans. He saw an assortment of fruits in a bowl with an envelope beside it. Dustin took the envelope after replacing the lid over the main course. He removed the contents of the envelope and read it.

Dear Dustin;

> *I assure you, first of all, that there is nothing wrong with this food. It has not been injected with any potions or chemicals. I have come to realize that my previous methods did not convince you to take the implant. I was overly concerned with saving your soul. You taught me that, Dustin. My friend, you take time to decide. Imagine the value of your life to others. If you accept the offer of the chip, perhaps together we can bring to the world a new method of convincing people in love rather than in hate.*

Your friend,
Dr. Cornelius Devlin

Dustin set the card and envelope down and sat in one of the four plush chairs arranged around the table. He stared at the silver setting for a few minutes. What would he have to sacrifice for this meal?

He decided that he would need his strength, so he ate an apple and an orange from the fruit bowl. He went into the bathroom and found it quite elegantly adorned. This is some fun house. From a room filled with torture devices to a dank cell, to a hotel suite. After brushing his teeth and showering, he went back to bed and slept.

The next time the door opened, it woke him. He looked up. He sat up as a servant in a tux strolled into the room and sat the silver setting on the table.

"Good day, Sir," he said.

He noticed the man said "good day." What time of day was it?

Dustin still had no concept of time as this "suite" was conspicuously void of a window or clock.

"Will there be anything else, Sir?"

"Yeah. Yes, there is something else. Could you have them bring the car around? I feel like a drive."

The man chuckled.

"Thank you, Sir," he said.

He turned and left.

The ritual continued with notes urging Dustin in the direction of the chip. Dustin could not tell how long it went on. He estimated two days of meals. Finally, Devlin entered with the goons.

"You still haven't asked for the implant," Devlin said as he sat in the chair across from Dustin.

Devlin poured himself a cup of tea. Two of the goons took the other two chairs.

"I've had a decidedly better offer."

Devlin took a sip of his tea and looked at Dustin. Dustin could tell that he was not happy. With a wave of his arm, Devlin cleared the table of the silver setting and sent it crashing to the floor. One of the goons raised slightly, grabbed Dustin by the hair and slammed his face into the table twice. Dustin had enough strength to possibly resist the assault, but it took him by surprise. The other man assisted in lifting Dustin from his chair and throwing him on the floor. Before he could get up, the two other goons stepped on his hands. Devlin knelt down and lifted Dustin's head.

"You caused a stir at the morning meeting, my friend. I tried torture and I tried love and mercy. The boys are getting bored and voted that it is their turn. Hey, this is a Democracy and I have to go with the majority.

"But I wanted you to be aware of the uselessness of the situation. I wanted you to be aware of the utter powerlessness of your God. You said 'ten days', right? Well this is day ten, my friend. I've decided to extend your stay."

Devlin stood up and two of the goons began beating him on the head and across the body with the rubber clubs while the other two ground their feet on his hands. They finally let him roll over so the could beat him across the knees and stomach. They hit him across the abdomen and the ribs. They hit his knees and head.

They were interrupted by a sudden explosion that shook the building. A couple of seconds later, an alarm sounded. The men ran out of the room. Dustin remained on the floor moaning. He finally decided to roll over and get up. When he did, he noticed that his tormentors left the door open. He listened and heard the fire fight.

Another explosion shook some pieces from the ceiling that fell on him. He had sense enough to realize that he was in danger. Dustin stood and carefully looked out of the door. He heard an explosion down the hall and looked. The doors at the end of the hall blew in and men poured in. It wasn't who he expected at all. Men of the militia group and Renegade Squad poured in filling the hall. In the lead was Paul.

Paul spotted him and it was apparent by his expression that he could not believe his eyes. He ran to him and grabbed Dustin's shoulder.

"You again?"

"Yeah. We've really got to stop meeting like this. But I have to say I'm really glad to see you."

"Can you walk?"

"Yes."

"Go back down the hall and out. It's clear. You can get help there."

"Okay."

Paul and his group continued on their way as Dustin followed instructions and walked into the cold night. Patches of stars fought against a waning moon and city lights for visibility. They were interrupted by the occasional black shape floating through the air.

Sergeant Jarvis spotted him first. He called out for a blanket and a medic and rushed to his side. William saw the exchange and ran to him, as well.

"What the heck are you doing here? Carole told us you left her at the house and then disappeared. Man, we were looking all over for you," William said.

"Is Carole all right?"

"Yes. And she is waiting for you," William smiled.

"Well, thanks for coming. You couldn't have chosen a more opportune time from my perspective."

"Fall back, now. There are some people who can help you."

Sparks suddenly erupted and people fell around them as a black Z-12 flew overhead firing. People were too busy firing at U.N. troops and helicopters to pay attention to Dustin. He moved through the firing crowd behind some of the vehicles. He ducked into an alley. Before he realized it, the gunfire was diminishing. He was in the dark and alone. He panicked and became disoriented.

Some U.N. soldiers spotted him and charged after him. He ran. Dustin managed to get himself into the bed of a truck and lay down. Amazingly, his pursuers did not even stop to check. He glanced up to see that they were now engaged with a group of militia men. He decided to lay back down and hope the truck would protect him from any stray bullets.

His side ached, but he did not think that his ribs were broken. Only bruised. His head ached as a result of being punched too many times. He thought his fingers might be broken, so he looked at his hands. He moved his fingers and was please to find that they were still in good order. His legs were in good shape as he could still run. How he managed to run this far was a mystery to him, but he was thankful for the mystery. He thanked this God that he, now, wanted to know.

Dustin heard the door to the cab open and felt the truck move slightly as the owner got in. The door slammed shut and the truck revved to life. He thought about getting out, but decided that the truck would remove him from the area. Given some distance, he might escape the city once more.

CHAPTER THIRTEEN

The truck stopped and the driver turned the engine off. The sudden stop woke Dustin. The driver got out and left the vehicle. His ribs did not ache as much and his hands felt better. Dustin's head still ached, but what was that ringing in his head? It wasn't a ringing, he realized. It was singing. A happy sound as if a thousand angels sung for joy. Dustin carefully got out of the back of the truck and looked up and down the street. There were U.N. troops and police harassing people for papers in the darkness. Yet, just down the block he could see a building lit up bright. It was from this location that the sound appeared to originate. He listened. No music, just the melodic sound of a choir.

Morning has broken,
like the first morning.
Blackbird has spoken
like the first bird,
Praise for the singing
praise for the morning
Praise for the springing
fresh from the word...

He noticed a fifth of bourbon on the bed of the truck. He did not know why he noticed it, but decided to use it. He took three swallows, then splashed some on his face and body. The alcohol burned the cuts in his face, but with his disheveled look, he hoped to appear to be just another rummy on the street. He walked toward the singing as two U.N.

troops walked toward him. He stepped aside, quickly, and kept his head down in submission. That seemed to appease the two men who went by him with only a comment about the stupid, drunk American. It seemed to please them that America was in such a state.

> *Sweet the rain's new fall*
> *sunlight from heaven*
> *Like the first dew fall*
> *on the first grass*
> *Praise for the sweetness*
> *of the wet garden*
> *Spring in completeness*
> *where his feet pass*

As Dustin continued toward the pleasant sound, his head cleared a bit. He began to recognize buildings and streets. It was the church to which Dustin went for advice. Now he understood why the priest stayed.

When Dustin stepped into the lights shining outside of the church, his eyes burned and tears flowed. For a moment, as his eyes were adjusting, it seemed that he was stepping onto a street of gold.

> *Mine is the sunlight*
> *mine is the morning*
> *Born of the one light*
> *Eden saw play*
> *Praise with elation*
> *praise every morning*
> *God's recreation*
> *of the new day...*

The doors were wide open and the sanctuary was packed. He entered and the ocean of people spread apart as if they were waiting just for him. They continued to sing and smile at him as he passed through the crowd. One face stood out. It was a sixteen-year old black youth. Dustin approached the boy in amazement. As he got closer, he saw his mother and two brothers. They saw him and smiled.

"Danny. Is it really you? I can't believe it? Where's your dad?"

The boys face became somber.

"He's dead."

Danny's mother added, "The police and those U.N. peace keepers broke in in the middle of the night. We were planning on being gone the next day. Dwayne was killed giving us time to get away. How we escaped, I don't know."

Dustin began to tremble and a tear fell down his cheek. He reached out and hugged Dwayne's wife and Danny.

"I'm so sorry I wasn't there to help."

"You did enough. What happened to you warned Dwayne of what these people are really like. If it weren't for you, we would not have been packed and ready to leave."

"We were told to come here," Danny interrupted. "To see him."

Dustin looked in the direction Danny pointed. The priest was defiantly there. His hair was as white as the robe he wore. The song continued as the people laid down in a large tub. The priest said something to them, then he dunked them. Dustin stepped in line.

When he got closer, he realized that they were being dunked in water. This was a baptism. Should he stay in line? He noticed that other people were still getting in line behind him. He looked back at the door and saw more people coming in. How many would this building hold? Certainly they had all ready exceeded the code limits. Still, it seemed that there was room for them. He noticed that the occasional U.N. troop would look in and sneer.

With a barely perceptible pause, the choir changed their song to Joy to the World. It was a Christmas carol that Dustin was familiar with. He seemed to remember his mother humming that tune all year around.

He abruptly found himself facing the smiling priest.

"Dustin. So glad that you arrived."

"Thank you, Father."

"The time for calling me *Father* has ended," the Priest replied. "Call me Herald. That is my given name. It is spelled h-e-r-a-l-d. Like the occupation. Not the new English spelling."

"Is that what you are? A herald?"

"We all have our job to do. In a few hours, this place will be burned to the ground and all of the people in it will be dead. Do you understand baptism?"

Dustin was surprised that the priest was so calm, even a bit pleased, about the fact that all of these people would be dead.

"I think so. I get baptized to show that I accept the Lord Jesus as my savior. I am 'buried' in the water to show that I am dead to sin. I rise again a new man cleansed of sin."

Dustin suddenly realized that he was using the personal pronoun. As if he were in need of this cleansing.

"You did read that Bible that I gave you."

"Not all of it. But apparently the important parts."

"Do you want to be baptized?"

"I haven't accepted Jesus as my savior," Dustin shook his head sadly.

"No time like the present."

Dustin fell to his knees more tired than anything else. He was in such pain. There must be a God. He would never have gotten this far in this environment by himself. Since he believed, now, that there was a God, he wanted to be a part of it. But he wasn't sure how to pray. The Priest just looked at him and smiled while the people in line went around him for their own baptism. All he could do was think to himself.

God. I'm sorry. I didn't know. I didn't know. Now that I do—I'm not sure if I'm doing this right, God. I want Jesus in my life. I believe in him and accept him. I believe that he spilt his human blood for my sins. Cleanse me, father. And forgive me.

A couple of people in line helped him to his feet. How did they know that he was done? They helped him into the baptismal pond.

"Do you accept Jesus and forsake Satan and all his works?" the Priest asked.

"I do, Herald. I do."

"Then I baptize you in the name of the Father, and of the Son, and of the Holy Spirit."

The singing became muffled as Dustin's head was dunked under the water. There was a darkness that frightened him. A darkness that surrounded him in the water and tried to close in on him. It seemed as though the lighter, warmer water pushed it away. The singing sprang to life as he was lifted from the water after what seemed like ten minutes. He expected to emerge totally healed. Yet, his ribs and head still ached and he had only limited use of his fingers. Herald apparently sensed his feelings and he and a couple of others lifted him out of the water.

"You are still human," Herald told him. "But you are no longer of the world."

"I lost my Bible. Do you have another."

Surprisingly, Herald laughed and patted Dustin on the chest.

"The word is now written in your heart, my boy. Keep it close and it will guide you."

Dustin did not understand, but nodded his head.

"Now, go, boy. In but a few days, you will see the word manifest once more. I wish that I could be there."

Dustin went to the door and down the hall—that he remembered from before—and exited into the courtyard. It was packed with people, as well. He wanted to stay and join in the singing, but saw the familiar face of a man who had donned a priestly robe. The man held another robe out toward him. Dustin could not believe his eyes.

"Raphael?" he said meekly.

He walked to the young man who simply smiled in return.

"You— You were dead. I saw you die in the explosion. You have to be dead."

"There is only one real death," he said still offering the robe. "Get out of those wet clothes."

Dustin stripped down, quickly, to his underwear and put on the robe. It was an amazing deterrent to the cold. Raphael turned and opened a back gate that Dustin did not know existed. As soon as they passed through the gate and closed it behind them, the singing all but stopped. It was too muffled to hear as if some force generated around the complex to hold in its joyousness. He was back into the evil.

They started to walk until a voice stopped them.

"You there! Halt!" a voice rang out.

Three U.N. soldiers approached them. Dustin ensured that the hood on the acolyte robe obscured his face from their vision just in case they had been informed to look out for him. The soldiers laughed when they saw the robes.

"Nothing to worry about here. Just a couple of peaceful priest," one of them jested.

The man struck Dustin in the ribs with the butt of his rifle. Dustin fell to his knees trying not to cry out. He did not want the man to know that his ribs ached so. It might tip him off to his real identity.

"Oh, sorry, there, buddy. I shouldn't have done that to a man of peace. You going to turn the other cheek?" he laughed.

"It is all right. I'll pray for you, my son. *Peace* on you. *Peace* on all of you, my sons."

One of the men might have caught on to his veiled obscenity as he started to reach down to lift the veil from Dustin's head. Dustin prepared himself for a fight. A vehicle screeched around the corner and stopped with its lights illuminating the scene.

"Hey, you men!" a voice called out. "What gives?"

"Just checking out a couple of priests," the first man reported.

"Well, get down to 23rd street. There is a mob forming. They need assistance."

"Yes, Sir!" the men replied.

The truck pulled away. One of the other men turned back to the priests and spoke.

"Your time is nigh," he said. "As soon as we get the official order, you will all be gone and we will have only one god."

The soldiers left to do as they were instructed.

"Raphael," he said, "I'm tired. I don't think I can walk anymore."

"That's all right. Just rest," Raphael said.

Dustin went to sleep right there without a thought to safety.

* * *

Dustin woke up and he realized that he was rolling around. He was becoming somewhat nauseated. He sat up and stabilized himself so that he could get a look around. He found that he was on a small yacht and that the coastline was slowly fading from view. He heard Raphael singing.

*"Sailing takes me away to where I've always heard it could
be.
Just a dream and the wind to carry me. And soon I will be
free."*

"What is that? Some sort of hymn?"

"No. It's Christopher Cross. But then, I do not suppose that you
were too interested in the oldies radio stations.

"What are we doing here?"

"Sailing. . ." Raphael started to sing.

"No, I mean where are we going? I've got to get back to Carole."

"She is fine. As for where we are headed, I don't know. I've never
sailed before. Thought I'd give it a try. You were injured and looked
like you needed some rest. I drove to the coast and bought us a boat."

"You drove. Without giving me a chance to protect myself."

"I've become much better, since then. It's a very limited means of
transportation, but—."

"And you bought a boat?"

"Yes. I gave a guy nearly a pound of gold for it. He might feel
cheated when he finds out that he only has a few days to spend it."

"The church and the priest?"

"To be absent from the body is to be present with the Lord," was
his only comment.

"Well I haven't sailed, either. How are we supposed to steer this
rig?"

"I don't intend to."

"How are we supposed to get where we are going? What if a storm
comes up?"

"He can still the waters. I'm sure that He can steer a boat," Raphael
argued.

Dustin thought for a minute.

"What a minute, here. I read that Jesus *rode* in boats, but he never
sailed them."

"Well, if you trust him enough, you can use his other mode of
transportation."

"What?"

Raphael pointed.

"The shore is that way. Start walking. Me, I'll trust his rigging."

"You know what you get when you give a donkey a diploma?" Dustin asked.

Raphael was confused. He thought for a moment. Then shook his head.

"No. What do you get?"

"A smart ass."

* * *

It was actually an amazing journey. Dustin counted fifteen days. The ocean was smooth. Even the daily rain squall that provided moisture did not churn up the ocean waters. Dustin adapted to the continual, slow rolling of the yacht more quickly than he thought he would. Each day, Dustin swooped a net through the water to bring up fish to cook. He was glad that there was a small galley in this yacht that Raphael bought. Dustin never could get into that Sushi craze.

As dawn broke on the sixteenth day, it silhouetted the shape of land in the distance.

"Where are we?" Dustin asked.

"Israel."

"*Israel*? But I thought—."

"Carole is fine. Will be fine. Life's good for her. Just follow the path that God sets, my friend."

"All right. But I just gotta know one thing. Who are you? Really? Are you what I think you are?"

"I suppose that it will do no harm to admit it, now. I am an angel of God."

"Then you lied to me?"

"When?"

"Oh, we're just guys," Dustin mocked.

"Now I'm going to delve into the finer point of the law. You never really asked *what* I was. You asked *who* I was. When we met you asked me what I *wanted* to be called and I said Clarence. You never asked for my real name. Technically, I'm good.

"Secondly, we are really just guys. We have certain abilities that God gives us to use and He directs us on how to use them. Just like you. You just have to listen harder. Bear in mind that we are not more important than you. Indeed, it is the other way around."

As they came closer, they could make out large warships. Occasionally, one fired off a missile to create some havoc in some unseen location. Drawing nearer and with the sun rising higher, they could see a flotilla of small cargo ships and yachts which had brought others from throughout the world to defend the tiny country of Israel. At least, Dustin hoped that they were pulling into the side that would defend Israel. The ships ignored them as they traversed the harbor. The yacht sailed up next to the dock and stopped. It was spooky, but Dustin was happy to get ashore. Dustin had never sailed, before, and he almost stumbled to the dock as he got out of the boat. Raphael stepped off the boat and spoke to him as he passed.

"You have to lose your sea legs. Just take it easy for a while."

When Dustin reached the end of the dock, there was an Israeli army sergeant standing there with a couple of armed men. He said something that sounded like gibberish to Dustin.

"Wait, wait. I don't speak Israeli."

"Are you medic, soldier or other."

"I guess I am soldier."

"That way, please," the sergeant said pointing toward a tent.

Dustin walked to the prescribed location and entered the tent. There were four women and a man behind a table lined with camouflage outfits, weapons and other equipment for the field. He stepped up to the table as the man spoke.

"Pant and shirt size?"

"Large shirt. Pants, thirty-four inseam and thirty waist."

The man had obviously been doing this for some time as he gave Dustin a strange look.

"All right. Thirty-two waist."

The man handed him pants, a shirt and a belt.

"You will have to tighten the belt. Next please."

He moved down the line and the next women gave him and Uzi, a belt outfitted with eight clips and two full canteens of water. He received a small pack which he would later learn contained field rations for four days, first aid kit, seven grenades and other necessities for combat. When he arrived at the last older woman he laughed.

"Wow. No background check."

Obviously she did not speak English. She just stared at him. Without being properly versed in English, she could not possibly understand the nuance of the joke. He was, of course, referring to the old United States concept of background checks before they outlawed the right to bear arms altogether. At least, he hoped it was because she did not speak English. He shrugged and left the tent.

When he stepped outside, he saw a sight that astonished him. The preacher from Quinden sat in back of a truck with other soldiers. The preacher's wandering eye caught sight of Dustin and he smiled.

"Hey!" he called and then pulled out the 9mm that Dustin had given him. "Thanks. I'll put it to better use."

"What are you doing here?"

As the truck started to pull away, the preacher yelled back at him.

"I'm correcting a mistake!"

The next two weeks were spent training and evaluating the recruits. The recruits were a rag-tag assortment of men and women from Africa, England, Germany, France, Russia, all of the Americas and from all points of the globe. About two-thirds of these recruits were Israelis returning to their homeland for the fight. Others expressed the idealistic notion that a victory, here, against the mighty armies of Pope Olivi, might inspire those in their homeland to fight for their freedoms. Then there were those, like Dustin, who had no idea why they wound up here or even what they were getting themselves into. While the State-controlled media and the loyalists to the Pope chanted the mantra, Who can make war against the armies of the Pope, there was no talk of defeat in this crowd. It was as if they never anticipated it possible.

The recruits were trained twelve hours a day. They were allowed one half-hour period in the middle of the day to eat and take a break. The rest of the day was yours to clean your weapons and uniforms for inspection the next morning. You could study any material that was given to you that day because you were expected to have it memorized by the next morning. You might be called in, during this time, for an evaluation conference with officers. There was, also, guard duty sometime during this off-time period every other day. Sometimes the recruits had to assist in cleaning the kitchen and preparing the meals for the next day. Then there was the daily barracks inspections that you had to prepare for. You had all of the off-duty time you needed to clean and prepare. When any and all of the aforementioned items were completed, you might even get a chance to squeeze in some sleep.

The training was conducted by twelve very experienced Israeli Army sergeants. The training sergeants had no compunction about getting physical to enhance their point. Every other day, or so, Israeli officers would come out and give instruction and watch some of the training sessions. The officers never spoke to recruits except during the evaluation conferences that you might have to attend.

The first day was spent learning a sign language that they had developed. One of the sergeants was known to speak perfect English, but he used sign to get the recruits used to it. The sergeant might raise a hand over his head so that everyone could see and point in a direction. He would walk and the recruits would follow. Two fingers pointing in a direction meant run. They learned later that four fingers in a particular direction meant attack in that direction. Most signals were self-explanatory. They would take a fist and put it to their mouth in a gesture that was similar to pulling the pin on a grenade. That meant to prepare a grenade. They would gesture in a direction three times and you were expected to throw the grenade in that direction on the third gesture. It was curious, at first, but it became clear that it was necessary. The Israeli army did not have time to teach every person a different language and the recruits certainly had no time to learn Hebrew. It had the added advantage of reducing chatter in a battle situation which increased the chance of surprise.

It was on the fifth day just prior to the half-hour rest period that the English-speaking recruits were called into an auditorium with a large television screen at the stage. The screen was all ready running a live news report direct from Jerusalem. In the courtyard of the Temple of Jerusalem, the two trouble-makers were standing beside Pope Olivi. Their hands were bound behind their backs and they just stared at the jeering crowd with smiles. Two Guillotines stood at the ready.

"Oh, man. Those guys are going to be sorry," Dustin accidently expressed his thoughts aloud.

He glanced around and the statement apparently caught the attention of Sergeant Shalev, one of the few English-speaking Israelis. Dustin smiled.

"You watch," he said.

Shalev returned his gaze to the screen as did Dustin.

Pope Olivi spoke in Latin. There was a over-voice translating his words.

"These things, these last remnants of the God you once worshipped afar, have said that I cannot save you from fire by opening up the sky and permitting the rain. I don't waste my power on parlor tricks. I use my power to love and care for those that choose to worship me!"

That drew a cheer from the crowd. Dustin chuckled and shook his head as the speech continued.

"Let us now see if their God, the God they are so obviously devoted to, can save them!"

Guards place the heads of the two men into the Guillotines. There was little resistance from the two men, which did not surprise Dustin. It was curious, though, that they let it get this far.

"Any second, now," Dustin murmured.

Two U.N. soldiers, void of the traditional black hood of executioner fame, walked to the right side of the Guillotines and stood waiting. The Pope gave his blessing and the men pulled a cord. The blades fell down quickly by the force of gravity. There was no instant shift in the gravitational pull of the earth. There was no interference that prevented the smooth operation of the blade. There were no laser beams. Just two heads rolling into the baskets to the delight of the cheering crowd.

Dustin stood and stared at the screen in disbelief. Olivi went to the basket containing the head of the man he knew as Christian. He lifted the basket up over his head and tipped it so the crowd could see it. The translator picked up the task of translating the Pope's Latin.

"As you can see, there is now only one savior on Earth for Earth. I will not fail you as others have failed you. I have won the right to be your savior!"

Glen Davis

The news report showed the crowd going crazy and hugging each other and kissing. Dustin sat back down still disbelieving what he just witnessed. Television was a lie. It just could not be true. The scene cut to a reporter interviewing members of the crowd. The first were two female and one male British citizen. Their faces beamed with delight.

"What do you think about what just occurred," the reporter wondered.

"It's wonderful," one of the women replied with glee.

"Yes. Now there is nothing left to prevent *Our Father* from crushing the last of the resistance and saving the world with peace and love," the young man added.

"What now?" the reporter prodded. "Will you go worship?"

"Right now we must go shopping," the woman who had been silent spoke.

"Yes," the man agreed. "I understand that there is a shop downtown that is all ready printing souvenir T-shirts and we simply must be among the first to get some."

"Yes," one of the women agreed. "We must send some to our friends in Lancaster."

The screen went blank and an Israeli Colonel stepped up to the stage.

"We wanted you all to see this," he began. "It was broadcast throughout the world on television and the Internet. The Olivi government wanted everyone to see this. Especially us.

"Now I am going to be very frank, with you. We are going against an insane, tyrannical and powerful evil. The whole of the Russian, Chinese, French, English—and the list goes on—armies are at the disposal of Pope Olivi. They are great in number and we are few. They are well-equipped. We are not. The only chance that we have is that God is on our side. That means that we must go into battle with a pure heart and a pure purpose.

"Any one who desires to leave for any reason will not be considered a coward. Now is the time to make that decision."

The officer paused and surveyed the men in the room. Finally he spoke.

"Sergeants, take charge."

The Top Sergeant stood and yelled, "Attention!"

The company of men stood and the Colonel left the stage.

"Dismissed!" the Sergeant yelled.

The men began filing out. As they did, Dustin noticed that Sergeant Shalev was assessing him.

A couple of people did leave the next day. The rest that stayed were in for intensified training sessions. It was apparent that they expected to be thrown into the Battle for Jerusalem, as it was coming to be know, quicker than they had anticipated. Dustin threw himself into the training. He trained with all the vigor that his hatred instilled. Two days after the event, Sergeant Shalev took him aside.

"I wonder," he began, "what causes such anger in a man. I saw you at the viewing, of course, you noticed that. Did you know one of those two men?"

"Yes. I did. I knew one of them."

"And you are bitter and angry over his death."

"Over the senseless death of two men."

"Over the death of this one man."

Dustin thought, for a minute, and finally admitted that was true.

"Why did you value his friendship so highly?"

The tears in Dustin's eyes were becoming difficult to control. His lips trembled.

"He taught me forgiveness," he said softly.

"And now, you would prefer vengeance. I must warn you, my friend, that vengeance is a double-edged sword. It can cut through the heart of your enemy. But it can also cut through your soul. It can disconnect your reasoning and cause you to make foolish mistakes.

"You remember the words of the Colonel. We must partake of this battle with a pure goal. Or all is lost."

"I've lost everything all ready. I lost my wife and child. I lost some friends. I've lost the only chance I had for love."

"Then if you lost your capacity for love and forgiveness, you have truly lost everything and I pity you. However, I believe if you reach deep down in your heart, you will find that you have lost nothing. It is only hidden. And it just might take a savior to find it for you."

Shalev departed leaving him to his thoughts.

CHAPTER FOURTEEN

*T*he next night, Dustin was awakened by the sound of jets thundering overhead shaking the barracks. He rose and started to dress and noticed that others were equally curious. They filed outside to find groups of attack helicopters moving inland. When air space permitted, a missile would proceed from one of the ships in the bay.

"Conrad! Get inside and wake everyone. Full battle packs," Shalev called to Dustin.

So it begins. Training was over.

Dustin and the others did as instructed. All two-hundred and fifty men were assembled and ready in less than one hour. Not a record time, but perhaps it was because the emotions ran the gamut from elated to terrified. Dustin felt driven by his hatred to attack, but a part of him wished all of this was a nightmare from which he would soon wake.

An Israeli soldier, with the emblem of a Major on his helmet, stepped up to the group. The man was big and muscular carrying his pack as if it were no more than the weight of a three-year old child. His voice was gruff and commanding, no real emotion.

"I am Major Caspi. We have to cut your training short. I am ordered to get you to the front which is now on the move. You are going into action sooner than we anticipated. We hoped to get you better trained for action. Once I get you there, you will be split up and assigned to more experienced troops, as best we can.

"While these men will try to teach you as quickly as possible, you must understand that there is a war on. We have basically given you as much training as we can. You should consider yourselves fortunate. Any recruits that might arrive, hereafter, will be handed a uniform, pack and a weapon and sent to the front.

"We may engage enemy troops along the way. My prayer is that this is not a devastating mistake.

"That being said, any one who wants to pull out for any reason may do so."

He began to speak again in several different languages. Dustin assumed that he was repeating the encouraging speech. One lad, who could not have been more than sixteen years of age, stepped out of the ranks. An older man soon followed. Two other men joined the group looking dejected.

"Do not despair, gentlemen," the Major smiled at them. "There are a number of reasons a man might quit. You may not feel ready. You may not feel adequately trained. Whatever the reason, you may be a danger to yourself and those around you. It is all right."

The major saluted them.

Caspi gave the order and those that remained were packed tightly into a caravan of trucks. The first part of their journey would be motorized.

The sun was rising as they finished the first leg of their journey. They would have to get through Jerusalem to get to the front. From here, marching would be the order of the day.

The group was broken up into groups according to their language. Sergeant Shalev would lead the English speakers. Kerem, the Germans and Russians, Yavin the Spanish-speaking—and so on. Major Caspi and Sergeant Navon took the speakers of all of the miscellaneous languages.

The mission was to break into groups and get through Jerusalem. There were to be no prisoners taken if you engaged. There was simply no way to transport or properly care for them. Intelligence reported that there were few U.N. troops in Jerusalem and most were employed in police duties controlling the crowd. Intelligence was wrong. About half a mile into Jerusalem, Sergeant Shalev ordered everyone to get down by hand signal. Every one ducked. Headed in their direction was a division of about fifty U.N. soldiers marching toward them followed by two Russian tanks. Shalev gestured to spread out and prepare a grenade. The Sergeant positioned himself so that most of the group could see him.

He gave the gesture and on the third gesture, most of the thirty grenades were lobbed into the air. About half reached the intended points and the grenades from the rest of the group followed. The U.N. soldiers were surprised and disoriented. The grenades had the desired effect of cutting them down to a manageable size. The militia group stood and opened fire. They were ordered to have their weapons on single-shot and to aim to conserve ammo. Most of the men remembered. In either case, much of the marching force was devastated and the rest ducked for cover. A sudden report came from the Russian tanks as they fired into the group randomly with their implanted machine guns. The two tanks lined up close to one another in the narrow street and were now firing. Dustin saw two or three men drop to the ground.

It was now a matter of taking out those two tanks and hunting down the remaining soldiers. Dustin moved tapping the shoulders of five men and they followed him quietly. They moved to position themselves in an alley on the flank of the tanks. As they moved, they took out four more U.N. soldiers. When they made it to the alley, they prepared grenades and stuck to the sides of the wall of a building and waited. When the tanks were in position, they tossed their grenades at the track of the tank closest to them, then ducked back into the alley for protection. They heard the explosion and peered out of the alleyway. The explosion ripped the track apart. The heavy wheels dug into the ground and stopped causing the front of the tank to veer in their direction. The track on the opposite side of the tank, surprisingly, caught the track of the other tank. The tank on their side sank further and it lifted the other tank causing it to roll over onto its side. As the men tried to escape from their iron coffins, the group moved in to finish them off.

Dustin emerged from the alley and caught the image of a blue helmet out of the corner of his eye. He swung the butt of his gun around and clubbed the soldier knocking off his helmet. He aimed his rifle to finish the job and paused. He was staring into the frightened eyes of a man of about twenty-years of age. He struggled to pull the trigger. He couldn't.

The man's head suddenly exploded and Dustin felt something hit him in the face. He lowered his rifle and wiped the blood of the man from his face and looked at it. He turned to see Shalev coming toward him.

"He was a young man. You did not want to cut him off in the prime of his life. That happens. Or, perhaps, you are realizing that hatred is not your best friend in battle. That is good. But, I will tell you, from experience, that delay is your worse enemy.

"If the situation were reversed, would he have delayed?"

"I don't know," Dustin muttered.

"Of course not. We *cannot* know the heart of another man. So don't take the chance. We were ordered to take no prisoners for a reason. Not out of hatred, but out of compassion. We simply cannot care for them. Don't prolong the inevitable by making them agonize."

Shalev walked away to survey the damage. Dustin followed. Eight men lay side-by-side with two corpsman attending to them. Several others stood waiting for attention with less serious wounds. Shalev walked beside a man with a chest wound. A medic was trying to calm him.

"Is there anything that you can do for him?" Shalev asked.

"Hardly, Sergeant."

"Then move on to the ones that you can help. We need to move."

Dustin was shocked. He laid down his weapon and knelt by the man. He was not much older than the young man Shalev had shot. Dustin looked up at Shalev angrily. Shalev simply smiled and moved on to check out the rest of the casualties.

When Dustin looked back at the man, his eyes were closed and his lips were moving. His chest heaved in an automated, but useless, attempt to fill his lungs with air. The man's eyes opened and he looked up at Dustin. He smiled and his face calmed. Finally, his body relaxed and stopped gasping for air. Dustin stood up and surveyed the man with tears in his eyes. Charles. Was that his name?

While he tried to remember, Shalev returned.

"I'm sorry that I have to be so rough, but we have to get out of here. You seem to move around a city very well."

"I was a cop," Dustin shrugged. "You learn how to move around in a dangerous city."

"Good. I need you to take two men to the next block and turn north. We have to pass by the temple, so I need you to assess the situation. Agreed."

Dustin nodded his head and looked at Shalev.

"Agreed."

Dustin volunteered two men and they moved in the ordered

direction sticking close to the walls of the buildings. Dustin looked up for any open windows that might contain snipers or other prying eyes. They successfully navigated the streets and went up the stairs to a building where they got a clear view of the plaza in front of the temple. Dustin extracted his binoculars and surveyed the scene. The bodies of the two men still lay on the ground in front of the temple. There were people dancing around the plaza taking breaks to run up and kick the bodies and spit on them. Dustin resisted the temptation to put his finger on the trigger of his weapon.

There was a sudden commotion and the music stopped. People were screaming and their dancing slowly subsided. Dustin strained to be able to get his binoculars in a position to view the disturbance. To his amazement, Raphael walked calmly through the crowd toward the plaza. A U.N. soldier stood in front of him to confront him. Raphael clapped two clinched fists on the sides of his head and the blue helmet collapsed under the strain. The soldier fell to the ground. As he continued, another soldier took aim to fire. With a wave of his hand something flew from Raphael's hand impaling the soldier in the chest.

Dustin put his binoculars away and turned to go to the stairs. One of the men stopped him.

"You can't go down there," he said.

"Listen. You two get back and report to Sergeant Shalev. Report that there are a few U.N. soldiers down there, but mostly civilian revelers. Now, go!"

The man shook his head and the two men went off to accomplish their task. Dustin followed them down the stairs and watched them for a moment. He turned and went toward the plaza. The revelers were now engaged in yelling obscenities at the intruder. They were too busy to interfere with Dustin as he moved up to get a clear understanding of what was going on. Pope Olivi was yelling at Raphael in Latin. Raphael calmly replied, in kind, and waved his hand. Olivi's behavior changed and he cowered down into a corner of the plaza. People were yelling at him to destroy the creature, but he stood fast averting his eyes from Raphael.

Raphael calmly, and respectfully, laid the bodies out on the plaza. He laid the heads, very gingerly, at the neck of the appropriate bodies.

He knelt between the two bodies and laid his hands on the stomachs of the corpses. He closed his eyes and looked skyward. As he opened his eyes, he began to glow. A light blue glow that spread and surrounded the bodies. To the amazement of Dustin, the two men sat up and the glowing slowly subsided. They stood.

There were screams of terror and anguish from the crowd as they looked on the astonishing sight. Some started to curse God and the creature that stood before them. The two witnesses began to glow, and Dustin knew what was coming. He ran from the plaza and ducked into a building just as the blasts began. He knew that there must be those strange, orange laser beams emanating from the two men. When the screams and the glowing subsided, he slowly rose up to peek through the window. There were piles of ash as far as he could see.

He slowly walked out of the building and toward the plaza. Christian and Raphael smiled when they saw him. He walked up to them and could only stare at them in astonishment.

"Raphael," he finally spoke. "You are an angel."

Dustin really believed that fact, now.

"Yes."

"Why didn't you tell me from the beginning?"

"Would it have mattered?"

"*Yeah*," Dustin replied.

"That is why I didn't tell you. You know, you are not supposed to depend on us to get through your miserable daily lives. That's what you have a God for. We are just the messengers."

"And Christian?"

"That, of course, is not my real name," Christian interjected.

Christian stepped off of the plaza and down on the street next to Dustin. He grabbed Dustin by the shoulder.

"You have grown so much over the last six months. You have overcome bitterness, hatred and vengeance. You have learned the power of love. And I dare say there might even be a little faith inside you," he smiled. "None of that would have been possible if we just gave you all of the answers. You had to make the right decisions. I can tell you that God all ready knew how you would answer."

"So there is none of that *free-will* crap that preachers have been spouting."

"Very much so," Raphael interrupted. "You see, God is the Alpha and the Omega. He was there at the beginning. He will be there at the very end of this whole affair. And he is here now. He knew every decision that you were ever going to make."

"Then why can't he just stop all of this?"

Christian smiled.

"There was a man by the name of Nathanael who sat under a fig tree. A disciple of Jesus came to him and told him that they had found the messiah. He did not believe Philip because he felt that no good could come out of the city of Nazareth. When Jesus saw Nathanael coming to him, he declared that Nathanael was an honest man not given to trickery or deceit to get what he wanted. Nathanael wanted to know how Jesus knew him and Jesus told him that before Philip brought him, he was sitting under a fig tree.

"Nathanael was stunned and said, '*Rabbi, thou art the Son of God; thou art the King of Israel*'.

"*Jesus answered and said unto him, 'Because I said unto thee, I saw thee under the fig tree, believest thou? thou shalt see greater things than these*'.

"Man is a stubborn animal. Sometimes he just has to see things for himself. Finish your journey, my friend. You shall, yet, see great things."

Their conversation was broken by the sound of men marching to the plaza. Christian turned and looked at them. He turned back to Dustin.

"This is the task assigned to Raphael. I must get back to my task."

Christian turned and walked toward the Pope. Dustin noticed that the other man all ready stood over him saying something in Latin. The Pope sat there on his knees in fear and crying.

Dustin followed Raphael toward the group and to the stretchers. Raphael stopped a man whose shoulder was bandaged. He closed his eyes and the strange blue glow surrounded his hands. The man was surprised and when Raphael stopped, the man began to move his arm around. He removed the bandages and the wound was gone.

Raphael continued touching and healing until he reached Charles and two other dead men. He just looked down at them. Dustin moved up behind him.

"Well?" he asked.

"There is nothing to do for these men," Raphael replied.

"What? You just healed a bunch of men. I saw you raise two guys that had their heads cut off! What do you mean you can't do anything for these guys?"

"I have my orders."

"So this is it for them? Their life is just snuffed out for nothing?"

Raphael turned to look at Dustin. His eyes, for the first time since Dustin met him, expressed a bit of anger.

"They have been rewarded," Raphael spoke softly.

Raphael turned away and walked down the path toward the area were the next great battle would occur. Some place Dustin never heard of called *Har Megiddo*. Dustin turned back to the plaza. The Pope and the two men were gone.

CHAPTER FIFTEEN

Dustin's group joined up with the others and they marched the rest of the way to *Har Megiddo*. *Megiddo* turned out to be a mountain surrounded by the *Jezreel* Valley. They arrived at dusk and were just able to make out the massive army that waited to attack. Just what they could see was unbelievable.

Dustin heard some one coming up behind him and turned to see the Quinden preacher.

"Well, well, well," Dustin said.

"I saw you standing here," the preacher held out his hand which Dustin accepted. "I hope I'm not disturbing you."

"Not at all. What is your name? I never had a chance to ask."

"George Calhon."

"How have you been, George?" Dustin said.

"You are looking out there and asking how I've been? I've been scared, thank you very much," he laughed.

"You seem to have a sunny disposition."

"I've read the last chapter. I know how the story ends. Pretty massive build-up, eh?"

"Yeah. Any idea how many?"

"Intelligence estimates about a million-and-a-half. I think they're being a bit conservative."

"How many do we have?"

"Oh, 'bout three-hundred-thousand."

"Three-hun—."

"Well, if each one of us takes out five enemy soldiers, we can all go home."

There was a commotion and men were yelling to come listen to a radio turned up as loud as possible. It was another news broadcast.

"Pope Olivi has fallen next to the Eiffel Tower," the reported announced. "Witnesses say that he was blessing people, then suddenly collapsed and, basically, disintegrated. There is wailing, here, that you cannot imagine. Herbert Thomas, SC news."

The broadcast switched to another report.

"Sev Levinson in Pompalona, Spain. I've heard the reports about the Pope in France and Germany, and there is mass hysteria, here, for the same reason. The term *Vanishing Pope* is being flashed across the Internet in reaction to the phenomena."

The voice of the anchorman interrupted the report. One could tell that he was weeping.

"We take you to Los Angeles for a special report from Tom Stenson. Tom."

"Here in L.A., the City of Angels, there are no angels tonight. Since the disappearance of the Pope, people have been cursing God. In retribution, they are breaking into the jails and prisons and trying to round up any remaining Christians to punish. It's pandemonium. Reports are that the safest places to be are in the rural areas were rebel Christian forces are in control. George."

"This is George Nelson. Everything seems to be falling apart. There is no word from the Temple in Jerusalem, but reports are that the two witnesses that were beheaded rose again. It sounds impossible, but reports have it that Pope Olivi is missing. It's hard to tell from the sketchy reports because we lost communications with Jerusalem completely. We have no information about the forces th. . ."

The voice faded out and the crowd booed and hissed.

"Sorry, people," the radio operator said. "We lost the signal."

The people started to return to their respective chores with a whistle. Others just relaxed. The conversation was brighter. It was as if they were preparing for nothing. It was over. The head of the snake had been cut off.

A sudden disturbance disquieted their jovial mood. A shriek in the night. They turned to see the fiery trail of a missile fired into the sky. Eyes followed the trail and people ran as it fell nearby. Another missile. The aim of the second was way off. There were fiery reports from the tanks which now moved closer to. Three or four shells hit the encampment, but caused little damage. Several other explosions went off around them. They were random shots. Perhaps the enemy was firing in hopes of getting a better idea of how they were situated. Maybe it was because their God was dead to them, now, so they had no direction. Could it be that they had just gone mad? What ever the reason, they would not go as quietly as everyone seemed to have anticipated.

The firing continued for about forty-five minutes. The enemy forces did manage to hit one of their tanks, a jeep and a tent. Amazingly, no one was around the jeep or in the tent. Everyone was lined up watching the pyrotechnic defiance.

The enemy attack on them ceased as formation after formation of jets flew overhead to deliver their own fervid blow on the enemy forces. Helicopter squadrons joined the attack. They flew lower and were more accurate with their shots. The rest of the night would be a battle between friendly aircraft, and the enemy knocking them down from the sky. It was easy to say that the enemy was suffering heavy casualties. Considering the size of the enemy force, it was easy for the jets and helicopters to inflict hundreds of casualties each time they passed overhead. It did make for a morale booster, though.

It was the hardware that concerned Dustin. Would they be able to take out enough of the armor and ammo to make a difference for their own depleted forces?

The enemy forces finally brought out their own aircraft. From a distance, the fire-fight had a sort of beauty. The rockets red glare. The bombs bursting in air. Pyrotechnics that would dwarf the greatest of Fourth of July celebrations. On the ground, Dustin realized it was a most different display. It was not a thing of beauty. It was a raining death. He considered the news reports that he heard this evening. People were going mad around the world. They were trying to wipe out any vestige of Christianity. If they succeeded, would the madness continue? How long before they turned on one another?

What would a man-made world be like?

Sergeant Shalev stepped beside Dustin and looked out on the display.

"We who are about to die salute you," he said.

Dustin looked at him curiously.

"That is supposedly what the Gladiators said in the arena, was it not? But, you know, one of them would always survive, according to legend. One would remain standing. Actually, Gladiators were expensive to train and maintain. It is believed that the old thumbs-up, thumbs-down signal was something that Hollywood added for effect."

"You must have been a soldier all of your life," Dustin shook his head.

"About eight months. I was a librarian before."

Dustin looked at him and laughed.

"No, I'm not kidding. The commander of the artillery during the *Revolutionary war*—what was his name? Henry Knox? A bookseller in Boston before the war. I must have read a hundred books a year for ten-years. When I got here, I told them what I know and *badda-bing badda-boom*. Oh, yes. I grew up in New York City. The New York City Public Library was my university. My parents could not afford college."

"Where are they now?"

"My father died when I was fourteen. I do not know where my mother is. I came home, one day, and the police were dragging her away. She would not get the chip, as I would not. I suspected that they were looking for me, as well. Jews were rounded up first, you know. I dropped my book and ran. I was scared. I sacrificed my mother so that I could live."

There was a tear in his eye and a slight tremble in his voice.

"There was nothing that you could have done. I know that from experience," Dustin tried to comfort him. "You would have been killed and that would have done us no good here."

"It's not that. It's just that . . ."

"What, then? What is it?" Dustin prodded.

"I probably own a hefty fine for that book I lost."

Dustin turned and stared at him. Shalev looked at him and smiled despite the effort to hold back the tears. Both men burst out in laughter.

"How do you do it?" Dustin finally asked.

"Do what?"

"This? How did you learn to forgive and get over the hatred."

"That took about six-months. I guess I just got over it. It wasn't helping me any. You have to, I guess, to survive. I wandered for awhile and flatter myself that God guided me here."

"Well, I gotta tell you, I think God guided us all here."

"Why? Why do you suppose that God would gather a meager force together which is bound to be slaughtered?"

"You said it yourself. Someone is bound to survive. Maybe he just needed witnesses. The Bible is full of references to two witnesses, right? Maybe that's me and you. Maybe we are to witness the power of God to any other survivors."

"I could write a book," Shalev laughed. "Well. Whatever the reason, I guess we should prepare. Get some sleep."

"You're kidding, right?"

Shalev shrugged and walked away.

Orders were finally being given throughout the ranks. The rays of the sun were just piercing the horizon to add to the eerie glow in the distance. It was enough to illuminate the mass that was moving toward them and the damage that was done in the night. The sun rose quickly and it was disquieting to see the tanks rolling around and over damaged equipment and corpses to reach them. When they were in range, the artillery began. Friendly shells added devastating blows to the air strike. Wave-after-wave of air and artillery strikes and still they kept coming. Apparently, they expected survivors, as well.

The friendly forces were organized into six waves. Dustin was part of the fourth. Every three minutes a new wave would be issued until there was nothing left but to finish the battle.

The final signals started. A loud horn blared so that all could hear it above the din of the firing artillery. The first wave of their forces ran out to engage the enemy.

Dustin had to wait until the third wave was ready to go before he could see the results. He looked over the shoulder of the man before him. Dustin did not know the remnants of one wave from the other, but there were still men and women up and fighting. The massive enemy force seemed to have slowed, but still kept coming.

The third wave got the signal and moved in. Some would throw grenades down the barrels of the oncoming tanks. Other groups set up with grenade launchers and mortars and did their best to stop the advance of the enemy force. Still, they kept coming. In a blood-lust worthy of *Atilla the Hun*, they kept coming. It was apparent that they intended to march straight through to Jerusalem destroying anything in their path.

Dustin's wave got the signal. He followed the rest of the screaming warriors into the battle. They waited to fire until they could tell they were only going to hit enemy forces. They stood behind defunct tanks for protection. They kept firing, one round at a time, inflicting casualty-after-casualty. Still, they kept coming and Dustin could not see the end of the enemy forces. They fired until they ran out of ammo or their barrels melted down. Then they tossed what ever remained of their grenades. Finally, they pulled their knives or used their bayonets to test the hand-to-hand skills they had learned.

Dustin heard the horn and knew that another wave was on the way. Wounded, falling back and trying to reach the aide stations, were gunned down as they ran. Enemy soldiers climbed the tank he was using for protection and jumped at him. He was amazed at his own ability to stave off the attacks. It was not a matter of heroism or any last great act of defiance. He just found himself engaged in surviving and ignored the rest of the battle.

His eyes were diverted to a flare in the sky. The sun was fully up into the sky, now, he realized, and he wondered why anyone would shoot a flare. The battle must have been raging for at least an hour. He looked at the other soldiers and all stopped and stared in similar dismay. The enemy soldiers were covering their eyes, to gaze into the light, or cowering in any corner they could find. Dustin found it curious that none of the friendly forces required such shielding to peer into the light. It was apparent that no one expected this.

Dustin looked skyward, once more. The light was spreading with a golden band spreading before it. It was so quiet that Dustin felt like he could hear a cough coming from San Francisco.

A figure emerged from the light riding a cloud as if it were a horse. Following him were thousands of men with swords.

"*That's my brother!*" one of the Israeli women said.

"Where?" a man asked.

"Right there!" she pointed and the man looked. "He was one of those feared kidnaped."

"How is that possible?"

"There is *Samuel*," another man pointed. "I recognize Samuel!"

The Israeli contingent was brightening up. Dustin quickly surveyed the area to find Shavel, but to no avail. He did notice that non-Israeli members of the friendly forces were regaining their senses and pulling back while the enemy glared in astonishment and anger. Dustin decided to join the sensible.

Dustin made it back to the friendly force encampment before the others and no one else was there. He looked back toward the fighting and the Israelis had joined into battle with the host from Heaven. The non-Israeli members stood watching the battle. Dustin smiled and poured himself a glass of water. He drank and realized that he could use a sandwich. He was rather too busy during the battle to be hungry, but now he was remembering that he did not even have breakfast. He looked around and spotted something laying on the ground. He gazed at it curiously.

He walked toward the small, white glob of substance about the size of a muffin. He picked it up and brushed it off. His fingers sunk into it, slightly, as if he were holding a large marshmallow. He sniffed it and it smelled sweet. He took a small bite. It was like nothing he ever tasted before. There was a sweetness to it, but it did not leave a sweet after-taste. It had a sturdier consistency than a marshmallow, but seemed to melt into his mouth. Even the small portion seemed to be filling him up.

"*You!*" he heard a voice.

He turned to look at the intruder and could not believe his eyes. There stood Devlin with T.O. close behind.

"What, now," Dustin whined.

"*You* did this!"

"Did what?"

Devlin stepped toward the battle and with a wave of his hand indicated the carnage.

"This! I had it all worked out. There would be peace. There would be plenty. I even gave you a god. And you, and Christians like you, and Jews destroyed it all!"

"Oh, that. Glad that I could be of service," he laughed.

The scientist turned out to be rather deft, for a geek. He produced a .45 ACP and fire two rounds into Dustin in a move that surprised even his cohort. Dustin put his hand on the wound and lifted it up. He looked at it and saw the blood. This was his blood. And this time he felt that the bullet struck a major organ.

He looked back at Devlin. Devlin, also, looked surprised as T.O. had come up behind him. Devlin turned around to look at T.O. and was desperately feeling around for the knife that was stuck into his kidney. He fell forward and lay silently on the ground. Dustin collapsed onto his back. He looked around and saw Raphael step up beside him. He did not kneel, but T.O. stepped up to him and did kneel.

"I'm sorry. I thought it was over, too. I didn't realize that he was going to do that. I hope that you can forgive me," T.O. said.

His voice was calm and even, but there was a repentant quality about it.

"I all ready have," Dustin said weakly. "Except—."

"Except what?" T.O. asked.

"Isn't the good guy supposed to kill the bad guy?"

T.O. smiled and stood. He looked at Raphael.

"Are you with this group?" T.O. asked.

"You could say that," Raphael said.

"Then, let me ask you something. Is there such a thing as redemption in this new order of things?"

"I am not a judge," Raphael shook his head. "But you can certainly ask."

T.O. nodded. He lifted his hand and displayed it to Raphael.

"Look, ma, no chip," he said.

T.O. turned and slowly disappeared in the distance. Raphael looked back down at Dustin and smiled.

"I don't suppose you are here to doctor me up," Dustin commented.

Raphael shook his head with a smile.

"Your task is complete. It's your turn to rest, now."

"And what was my task?"

"Do you remember a little boy in a battle a month or so ago? You told him that God would not provide a shield that would keep the bullets from hitting him? He did. It hurts to be a shield, doesn't it?"

"That's it? My whole life was centered around being a shield for one little boy?"

"That little boy was a very special friend of the Lord."

"Why didn't I die at that time?"

"Apparently, you needed some time to sort things out. Maybe God was giving you time. I didn't write the plan, my friend. I cannot even tell you where you are destined from here. I'm not the judge."

"I don't understand this. Why didn't God just protect the boy by his own hand? Lift him out of the way, or something?"

"You remember what the Bible said about storing up treasures in heaven? You did not expect to get paid for doing nothing, did you?"

"And now, you are here. Why, if not to save me?" Dustin asked the angel.

"I am here to comfort a dear friend. Someone who taught me a few things," Raphael smiled.

Dustin looked into the eyes of the angel. They sparkled. A tear finally broke the dam and streamed down his cheek. But it wasn't a sad tear. It was the tear of an angel. Dustin laid back quietly and looked up into the clear blue sky one last time.